Milo March is a hard-drinking, womanizing, wisecracking, James-Bondian character. He always comes out on top through a combination of personality, bluff, bravado, luck, skill, experience, and intellect. He is a shrewd judge of human character, a crack shot, and a deeper character than I have found in most of the other spy/thriller novels I've read. But, above all, he is a con-man—and a very good one. It is Milo March himself who mak⌐⌐ the series worth reading.

—Don Miller, *The Mystery No*

Steeger Books is proud to reissue twen⁺   ⌐d stories by M.E. Chaber, whose Milo March №   ⌐inute action and breezily readable entertainmℇ

Milo is an Insurance Investigator whᴜ   ⌐h cases. Organized crime, grand theft, arson, suspicious disapp⌐ , murders, and millions and millions of dollars—whatever it is, Milo is just the man for the job. Or even the only man for it.

During World War II, Milo was assigned to the OSS and later the CIA. Now in the Army Reserves, with the rank of Major, he is recalled for special jobs behind the Iron Curtain. As an agent, he chops necks, trusses men like chickens to steal their uniforms, shoots point blank at secret police—yet shows compassion to an agent from the other side.

Whatever Milo does, he knows how to do it right. When the work is completed, he returns to his favorite things: women, booze, and good food, more or less in that order....

THE MILO MARCH MYSTERIES

The Flaming Man

KENDELL FOSTER CROSSEN
Writing as
M.E. CHABER

With an Afterword by
KENDRA CROSSEN BURROUGHS

STEEGER BOOKS / 2021

PUBLISHED BY STEEGER BOOKS
Visit steegerbooks.com for more books like this.

PUBLISHING HISTORY

Hardcover
New York: Holt, Rinehart & Winston (A Rinehart Suspense Novel), February 1969. Dust jacket by Pete Plascencia.
Toronto: Holt, Rinehart & Winston of Canada, 1969.
London: Robert Hale, 1970.

Paperback
New York: Paperback Library (63-353), A Milo March Mystery, #9, June 1970. Cover by Robert McGinnis.

ISBN: 978-1-61827-572-1

For Louise Waller

Dear Louise: "Youse is a good kid."
M.E.C.

CONTENTS

ONE

It was late spring in New York City. The weather was already a little sticky. Everyone was thinking about getting a place on the beach for the summer or putting in more air-conditioning. I was no exception. My bank account was. It looked as if the Great Society* had never heard of me.

When the hot weather starts, all the rats—four-legged and two-legged—begin coming out of the woodwork and the sewers. There were rumblings and threats of riots. Murder and assassination (a political nicety for "murder") were on the increase. Every big city was in heat, and violence was the male dog in search of the bitch.

Me? I'm March. Milo March. That's what it says on the door of my office on Madison Avenue. It also says that I'm an insurance investigator. I wouldn't have been sure if I hadn't read it when I came in—business had been that bad for a few months. I was almost ready to believe that everyone had become honest and decided not to cheat the insurance companies anymore. Almost—but not quite.

I opened a desk drawer and took out a bottle of V.O. I lifted it and looked at the contents. It was almost as low as my bank account. I poured a drink anyway and tucked the bottle back

---

* President Lyndon Johnson's program to eradicate poverty in the U.S., initiated in 1965. (All footnotes were added by the editor.)

in the drawer, sipping the drink slowly. I thought of picking up the morning newspaper, but rejected the idea. Then the telephone rang. I thought quickly before answering it. The bills were all paid, so it couldn't be a creditor. I picked up the receiver and said hello.

"Milo?"

I recognized the voice. It belonged to Martin Raymond, a vice-president of Intercontinental Insurance. Most of my business comes from them. Things were looking up. I reached into the drawer and patted the V.O. bottle.

"I think so," I said. "I'm never sure until I've looked in the mirror, and I haven't had the courage to look this morning. How are you, Martin?"

"Great," he said. His voice dripped with the molasses of clean living. The whole act was a mirage, but he had to keep up the image. "Do you have time to do a little job for us?"

"It all depends on the size of the job," I said carefully. It never paid to be eager with Martin. "You know I can't stand those one-night stands."

He laughed, just to show he appreciated me. "Well, it's slightly bigger than that. Why don't you run up here and we'll try it on for size?"

"I forgot my running shoes today, but I'll slip downstairs and catch the first milk train that comes along. Don't give away the store before I get there." I put down the receiver.

Intercontinental owns their own building on Madison Avenue only a few blocks from my office. It's one of those modern structures, all glass and steel, with a few stones looking as if they'd been added as an afterthought. I walked to it and took the elevator to the executive floor.

When I stepped out of the elevator, I was ankle-deep in dark blue carpeting. I didn't even think about it. My attention was on the vision in front of me. This one was a blonde, but it didn't make any difference; she came from the same neighborhood as the other receptionist—about 38-24-36, a nice neighborhood no matter how you looked at it. I often wondered if they had a vice-president whose sole duty was to find and hire the receptionists. Lucky man.

"May I help you, sir?" It was the blonde interrupting my thoughts.

"Sure," I said. "What time do you get off work?"

A smile started to tug at her mouth, but she pushed it away. "Just in time to meet my husband. ... Whom did you wish to see?"

I glanced at her left hand. No rings. "You'll never get to heaven," I said, "telling those little white lies. Oh, well, I'll see Martin Raymond—but he'll be a poor substitute."

This time she did smile as she reached for the phone. "Who shall I say is calling?"

"Let's surprise him. ... No, I guess Martin wouldn't go for that bit. Just tell his secretary that there's a man here to pick up his Social Security in cash. She'll know who it is."

She was puzzled, but she picked up the phone and repeated what I'd said when she reached Martin's secretary. She was smiling when she replaced the receiver. "You may go in, Mr. March."

"Thank you," I said. I walked to the door, then looked back.

"You'd better get rid of that husband. I don't think he's any good for you—and you could help me spend Intercontinental's money." I stepped through the door and walked down the corridor, wading through more plush carpet.

Martin's secretary looked up and nodded for me to go into his office, so I opened the door and entered. It looked like a vice-president's office. It was furnished with antiques that had been altered to make them functional. An early American cupboard was now a liquor closet. A cobbler's bench held sunken ashtrays, as well as cigarettes and matches.

"Milo, my boy, how are you?" Martin exclaimed. Suddenly I was his long-lost brother, so I knew it couldn't be an easy case.

"Exhausted," I said. "It was that long hike through the jungles."

"That's my boy. Anything for a laugh. Help yourself to a drink."

"I thought you'd never ask." I splashed some V.O. in a glass, and added a cube of ice from the lower part of the cupboard, while thinking that Martha Washington never had it so good. Then I went over and sat down next to the desk.

"How much did you pay for the carpeting in the corridor and the reception room?"

He looked surprised. "I don't know. Why?"

"I was just thinking that you could have saved a lot of money and gotten the same results by covering the floor with about three inches of Jell-O."

It took him about a minute to realize it was a joke, and then he laughed heartily. That was one thing about Martin

Raymond—he didn't have a sense of humor, but he had an instinct for knowing when he was supposed to laugh, and he always put on a good show.

I lit a cigarette and waited for him to finish the scene. "What's the case?" I asked then.

He immediately became all efficiency. "Fire. I suppose you've been reading the newspapers?"

"Of course. I never miss Dick Tracy. After all, we're more or less in the same business. Actually, I feel closer to Fearless Fosdick because he's also underpaid."

He gave a hollow laugh. "You underpaid? At three hundred dollars a day and expenses!" He pulled himself together and got the business look back on his face. "A man named Harry Masters. Lived in Los Angeles. President of a large corporation with holdings all over the city. Among other things, the corporation owned a fairly large building in southeast Los Angeles. There were two stores on the ground floor. One sold TV sets, radios, record players, that sort of stuff. It was owned by Masters and run by his brother-in-law. The other was a clothing store leased to a local merchant. The rest of the building consisted of offices. I understand the occupants were mostly lawyers, doctors, and dentists who worked in the community. One floor was occupied by the corporation, although they had several other offices around the city. During the riots a few days ago, it was burned down."

"Somebody dropped a cigarette, I suppose?"

"Molotov cocktails," he said grimly. "I don't know how many. The building was completely gutted, however."

"Insured, I presume?"

"Yes. By us. For two million dollars."

"Who gets the bread?"

"The corporation."

"If it was burned down by the rioters, don't you still have to pay?"

"I think so," he said.

"And you want me to go out there and smell around. You have a nasty mind, Martin. You think maybe someone burned it."

"It's always possible," he said. "There were also three people who were trapped in the building and died there."

I lit another cigarette. "So the plot thickens. Who were they?"

"Identification is not yet certain, but it is believed that two of them were Masters and his brother-in-law and the third one was the night watchman."

"Also insured?"

"I don't know about the watchman, but we carried policies on the other two men. There are two policies on Masters. One for two hundred thousand dollars, which his wife will collect—if he's dead. Another one for five hundred thousand dollars. The corporation is the beneficiary. The brother-in-law had a policy for fifty thousand dollars, which goes to his sister, Mrs. Masters."

"So we have two million, seven hundred and fifty thousand dollars," I said. "A tidy little sum. Do you have a concrete reason for being suspicious, or is it just your nasty thoughts?"

"There is no evidence," he said slowly, "but there's something wrong about the case. I can feel it. You know about that."

"I know," I said. "Is that the whole story?"

"There's more information in the file. My secretary has one for you. I—I suppose you want some expense money?"

"That's the name of the game, Martin. You can't expect me to do my best on bread and water."

"It's not the bread and water, it's the martinis and the girls. Will five—" He saw my expression and broke off. He sighed. It sounded as if he'd just been told he had only two weeks to live. "All right. My secretary will see that you get a thousand dollars. But try to make it last. You have no idea how the board complains about your expense vouchers."

I smiled at him. "I have an idea. I also have an idea that they forget about it when I save them a few million dollars. And in this case, what happens if the thousand dollars doesn't last?"

He sighed again. "Call me, and if you seem to be getting anyplace, we'll send you more."

"You're all heart," I told him.

I went out, stopping at the secretary's desk. "Hi, sweetheart. Want to run away with me?"

"I could afford to, on what you usually con him out of," she said. She handed me a manila envelope. "Here's the file on the Masters case. How much did you catch him for this time?"

"A thousand dollars."

She shook her head. "You're really wasting your time, Milo. You should go after the big con rackets instead of this small change." She scribbled on a piece of paper, signed her name, then pushed it across to me. "Take that to the cashier. You should know the way; you've been there often enough. And don't spend it all on that blond receptionist before you get out of the building."

"Jealous," I said.

I took the slip and made my way to the cashier. Two minutes later I had a handful of hundred-dollar bills. They warmed the cockles of my heart.

On my way out I gave the receptionist a smile calculated to make her regret that she had not accepted my suggestion, and stepped briskly into the elevator. When I was back on Madison Avenue, I looked at my watch. It was still too early for the good restaurants to be open. I did find a bar that was open, though, had a drink, and broke one of the big bills. Then I took a taxi down to the Blue Mill Inn on Commerce Street in the Village. Alcino was just starting to work back of the bar, and I ordered a dry martini. It was perfect, as they always are there.

After a couple of sips, I went to the phone booth, made a reservation on a flight to Los Angeles, then called my answering service and told them I'd be out of town for a few days. I went back to the bar, finished my martini, and had two more. Then I ordered a rare steak with a salad. I made it perfect with coffee and brandy.

Later I strolled up to my apartment on Perry Street and packed a bag for the trip. I set the clock and took a nap. When I awakened, I had just enough time for a cup of coffee with a shot of V.O. before I called a taxi to take me to Kennedy Airport.

I picked up my ticket, had one drink in the bar, and boarded the jet. We took off a few minutes later and I waited patiently while the Captain made his little speech over the intercom, then until the stewardess came around.

"I'll have a dry martini," I told her, "and go light on the dryness."

I said it even though I knew that the martinis were already mixed and sealed in a little bottle. All the girl did was open the bottle and pour it into a glass.

"Yes, sir," she said.

She came back a few minutes later with my drink. "I hope it's dry enough, sir." She was going to play it straight.

I took a sip and frowned seriously as I tasted. "Excellent," I said. "Give my compliments to the company that bottles it." We both had a good laugh over that. "And bring me another one," I added.

She looked a little doubtful, but she got it.

I opened my manila envelope from Intercontinental and took out the file. I read all of it, but there wasn't too much to add to what Martin had told me. The name of the brother-in-law was there, Larry Beld. There was also a report on Masters, which showed that he was a swinger. He and his wife had been married for thirty years and had no children. He always had at least one girlfriend somewhere nearby. He also liked to gamble and usually went to Reno, Nevada, at least once a month. Despite all this, his corporation was very solvent. The business had started as a small company making belts. At the time the report was made out, they were still in the belt business, but were also involved in real estate, and the manufacture of radar equipment for the government, and of radio and TV parts. They owned a number of shops in Los Angeles and kept a few fingers in other pies.

That was about it. There was nothing to indicate that Masters himself was in financial trouble. He spent a lot of money, but he made even more. He'd been playing footsie with a variety of girls for years, but there was no evidence that his wife or any of the girls objected.

It was like most of the cases that came my way. If there was going to be anything to work on, I'd have to dig it up myself. So I put away the file, finished my second martini, and went to sleep.

A few hours later the big plane went into a glide for International Airport. I knew it was already dark in New York, but here the sun was reflecting brightly from the Pacific Ocean. We came down in a smooth landing.

I went into the terminal, claimed my bag, reset my watch, and got a cab. The driver took me to the Continental Hotel. It made me feel I was being loyal to Intercontinental.

After I'd checked in at the hotel and settled in my room, I called room service and ordered a bottle of V.O. and a bucket of ice. I unpacked my suitcase, and by that time the waiter was knocking on the door.

As I made a drink, I considered what to do. Back in New York it was dinnertime. Here it wasn't—though my system hadn't accepted that yet. But it was still too late to start working. I picked up the phone and called a car-rental place I always used when I was in town. They were open and promised to deliver a car to me within a half hour.

I sipped my drink and finally decided I'd go down to Hollywood for a few drinks, and then pick a place to eat. I took a shower and changed clothes. I'd timed it perfectly. The phone rang and the desk clerk told me my car was ready. I went down and signed for it, got in, and started driving east.

I had several favorite bars in Hollywood, but I had decided I would go to one that I'd discovered the last time I was here—the Casa Del Monte on Hollywood Boulevard and Gramercy. It was run by Leonard Del Monte. Everything about the place was just enough out of focus to make it interesting.

I parked the Cadillac on Gramercy and went into the bar. It was so dark inside that I had to stand still for a minute so that my eyes could adjust. Then I moved over to a stool at the bar. There were seven or eight people sitting there and the owner was serving. He was talking to the other customers, moving back and forth in a sort of rhythmic step that reminded me of the way Bojangles Robinson used to dance. I remembered that nearly everyone called the owner Bo instead of using his real name, and that was probably the reason.

He looked up, saw me, and came down, still keeping time to the music from the jukebox.

"Hello, Bo," I said.

He took a closer look at me. "Hi," he said. "You're March, aren't you? Milo. You were here a few months ago. How's the action in New York?"

"The same as everywhere. You throw down your chips and they pull them in."

"Yeah," he said. "Still drinking the same? Gin and grapefruit juice?"

"Sometimes, but I think I'll have a martini now."

He mixed one swiftly and poured it. "This one's on me." He poured himself a shot of brandy and lifted his glass. "Glad to see you back. Going to be around long?"

"I don't know. I'm here on business. It all depends on how that turns out."

"I remember," he said, snapping his fingers. "You're an insurance eye. Going to send somebody to the bucket?"

"If I'm lucky. I read that you had a pretty bad riot out here."

"Yeah. It seems to be over now, but you never can tell. We didn't see any of it up here, but a lot of people were pretty nervous."

Another customer came in and he moved over to wait on him. I had two more martinis and decided I could break down and have dinner. I told Bo I'd see him again, and left. I drove up to Fairfax and stopped at a restaurant called The Jade Lady. I had a wonderful Chinese dinner and then drove back to my hotel.

I had a couple of drinks in the bar, bought a paper, and went up to my room. There were still a few emaciated ice cubes left, so I undressed, poured myself a drink, and stretched out on the bed. After I'd read the newspaper, I turned on a TV news broadcast. Everything was relatively quiet in the southeast section of Los Angeles, but it was obvious that people were still a little edgy. I turned off the TV and went to sleep.

It was early when I awakened the next morning. I phoned room service and ordered tomato juice, scrambled eggs and toast, a pot of coffee, and some ice. When they came, I had my usual morning drink and then enjoyed the breakfast. I had another small drink with my cigarette. Then I shaved, showered, and got dressed. It was time to go to work.

My first stop was to look up the records on Belters, Inc. There were some interesting things about it. Harry Masters was the president, but he held only 10 percent of the stock. His wife, Alice Masters, was the vice-president and also owned 10 percent. Larry Beld, the brother-in-law, didn't hold any office, but did own 5 percent of the stock. Someone named Frank Jeffers was treasurer, with 5 percent. A Kitty Harris had 19 percent. But the most interesting name was a Sherry LaSalle, who was the secretary of the corporation and held a tidy 51 per cent of the stock. I was going to look forward to meeting Sherry.

Next I drove to detective headquarters. I told my troubles to a desk sergeant, who finally consented to phone a lieutenant. Two minutes later I was knocking on an office door. A voice told me to come in.

The lieutenant was a big man, probably about fifty, who looked as if he'd been working straight through for about a week. His eyes were bloodshot, his suit wrinkled, and there were cigarette ashes all over the desk and his clothes.

"You're March?" he asked. "Let's see your ID."

I handed him a wallet which contained all my identification cards and waited while he went through it. Finally he tossed it on the desk where I could pick it up.

"A big man, huh?" he said. His voice was flat, so it was impossible to tell whether he was being ironic or hostile or merely indifferent. "Private detective license in New York and California. Gun permit in both states. Member of the

Footprinters.* Sit down. It makes me tired just to look at anyone standing."

I took the chair next to his desk. "Not a big man, Lieutenant. Just a guy doing his job. I don't make them. I just work at them when I'm told to."

"Going to come out here and solve all our little problems for us, huh?"

I shrugged. "I'm only interested in one tiny part of your problems. I'm also well aware that you probably haven't been to bed for several days, that the work is piled up over your head, and that you wish to hell that I'd go visit Disneyland or take a tour of Death Valley. I'll try not to take up too much of your time."

He sighed. "Yeah, it's been a little hairy around here. Sorry if I'm jumpy. Tell me what you want and I'll help you if I can."

I took out a sheet of paper and placed it in front of him. "I'm interested in that building, which was one of those burned."

He squinted at it and then stared at the wall for a minute or two. "Yeah," he said finally, "I remember that one. It was the Belters Building. When the firemen finally dug their way through it, there were three roasts in what was left."

"Identification?"

"Not very good, but about as good as we'll ever get. We believe they were—" He broke off and looked in one of the folders on his desk. "Harry Masters, who owned the building; Larry Beld, his brother-in-law who ran the TV store on the ground floor; and a colored watchman named Bob

---

* The International Footprint Association, or Footprinters, is dedicated to cooperation between everyone involved in law enforcement and all law enforcement agencies, as well as private citizens and professional people.

Summers. We have reason to believe that they were all three there that night, and the three bodies roughly correspond to the sizes of the men. That's all we have, and it'll be about all we get."

"What about dental identification?"

He shook his head. "No dental records have yet been found for Beld and the watchman. Masters wore false teeth—uppers and lowers."

"Didn't you find them?"

"No. We also didn't find any belt buckles. That was an all-out fire, March. By the time it was washed down, there was nothing left but the concrete shell and several feet of ashes, which had once been the floors, the furniture—and three bodies."

"I understand," I said, "that the fire was started by Molotov cocktails tossed through the windows on the first floor. To do that much damage there must have been some gasoline spilled around on other floors. Did you find any evidence?"

"No. Where were we going to find it—in the ashes? The Arson Squad sifted through everything and found nothing, not even any traces of gasoline thrown into the two stores on the ground floor."

"That's all?"

"That's about it," he said heavily. "And you'll have a lot of fun trying to find out who set that building on fire. There were quite a few people running around with torches that night. Going to cost your company much?"

"Almost three million dollars."

"That's a nice round sum. Well, you've got plenty of company." He managed a slight smile. "Sorry I can't be of more help, March. I can't seem to even help myself very much."

I took the hint and stood up. "Well, thanks a lot, Lieutenant. If I stumble over anything, I'll let you know."

"You do that," he said.

I could tell by the tone of his voice that he didn't think I'd do anything but fall on my face. I let it go at that and walked out.

I drove down to the riot area. It was quite a shock to see all the burned and scarred buildings. There were still plenty of police around, outnumbering the few sullen-looking Negroes on the street. I parked near what was left of the Belters Building and studied it. The Lieutenant was certainly right. It had been completely gutted. I walked around it. The view was the same from all sides. As I came back to the sidewalk, a cop lumbered up to me.

"Looking for something, bud?" he asked.

"Yes," I said. "A building that isn't here now."

He frowned. "What are you? Some kind of nut?"

"No. Just a man looking for yesterday's illusions and today's realities."

He got hung up on that one and decided to skip it. "Well, this ain't a very safe place for a white man to be. If you ask me, you'd better get back where you came from."

"But I didn't ask you, officer," I said gently. "It may be slightly bruised, but I think this is still the home of the brave and the land of the free. And I intend to stroll around for a bit. Just think of me as Diogenes without a light to aid my search."*

"Huh?" he said.

But I was already walking down the street. Most of the places of business were closed, many still bearing signs that read: *Owned by a soul brother.* But finally, about two blocks away from where I was parked, I found a bar that was open. I went inside.

There were maybe a dozen black men at one end of the room and a black man behind the bar. I stopped at the end nearest to the door and waited. The other customers had been drinking in silence or had stopped talking the minute I entered.

I waited patiently while the bartender shuffled his feet and pretended not to see me. Finally he tired of that game and came up to where I stood. "Yeah?" he said.

"I'll have a bourbon with water backed."

He scowled. "I ain't rightly sure we got any."

"Meaning you don't want to serve me?" I asked. "On what grounds? I'm not drunk. I'm not disorderly. I don't think the California ABC would like it."

He chewed on his lower lip for a minute, then shuffled off and came back with a shot glass and a glass with water in it. He poured the drink.

"Give the bar a drink," I said.

"How do I know you're going to pay for it?"

---

* Diogenes, the Cynic philosopher of ancient Greece, is said to have walked around with a lantern in broad daylight; when asked why, he said he was searching for an honest man. In other words, honest people are so rare that it takes an extraordinary effort to detect them.

I took out a ten-dollar bill and put it on the bar. He turned and served drinks to the others. He came back, took my bill, and rang up ten dollars. He didn't bring any change. I ignored that and sipped my drink. When I'd finished it, I rapped gently on the bar with an empty glass. He came up and refilled it. I gave him a dollar and he rang it up. Again no change.

I was halfway through the second drink when I saw one young man detach himself from the group and walk toward me. I couldn't tell whether he was coming to me or leaving the place, but I looked him over. He was young, maybe twenty-four or twenty-five, with a dark, handsome face, on the husky side and well dressed. He came to a stop about a foot from me.

"Hello, Whitey," he said.

I looked around. "Hello, Blackie."

There was a faint glint of humor in his eyes as he stared back at me. "Are you fuzz?" he asked.

I shook my head. "I'm allergic to fuzz. Even a peach makes me break out in a rash. Besides, I'm not strong enough to carry all that tin around with me."

"Then what are you doing here?"

"Having a drink," I said mildly. "Will you join me?" He hesitated for a minute, and then nodded. The bartender must have been watching, for he came right up. He filled my shot glass and then served my companion. I noticed he got a good brand of Scotch. I put two dollars on the bar and watched the bartender ring up the whole amount.

"I'd still like to know what you're doing here," my companion repeated.

"It's a funny thing," I said, "but I was asked pretty much

the same question by a police officer up the street. I'll tell you the same thing I told him. Just think of me as Diogenes without a light."

He smiled slightly. "It's pretty dark around here."

"I learned Braille in my youth."

"You'll need more than that, Whitey."

"Maybe." I lifted my glass. "To your good health. My name is Milo March. What's yours?"

He hesitated only a moment. "George Carver Henderson."

I nodded gravely. "A good name. But why did they leave out the Washington?"

That surprised him. "You know about George Washington Carver?"

"Yes. When I was fairly young, I developed the disgusting habit of reading."

"Well, my father was a great admirer of Carver, but I guess he thought that 'Washington' would be piling too much on my thin black shoulders."

"I can see that," I said. "And what is your contribution to the soybean culture?"

This time he really smiled. "I can't say much except that I've liked the soybean products I've had in Chinese restaurants."

"That's good. And what do you call a Chinese? Yellowy?"

Some anger showed in his eyes. "The Chinese are also a colored race."

"Isn't everyone? There is no such thing as a white race even though white is also a color. Frankly, I consider myself to be pleasingly pink."

He laughed. "Okay, so you're outtalking me. But don't you know it's dangerous to be down here just now?"

"It's dangerous to take a shower. What am I supposed to do, scrub myself with sand? It hurts."

"And you're not wanted," he said with some feeling. "Haven't you noticed that you don't get any change when you buy drinks?"

"I noticed. It makes me feel safe. If I get a mickey, I feel certain it'll be a good brand."

He laughed again. "Man, you break me up. If all of you Whiteys were like this, we wouldn't be able to fight back. We'd be too busy laughing."

"I keep telling you," I said patiently, "that I'm not called Whitey. I'm either Milo, or, if you prefer, Pinkie. I'm not sure I like the last name, but at least it's accurate. As a matter of fact, you're not really black. Maybe I should call you Brownie."

"Man, you're too much." Then the smile left his face. "But I still want to know what you're doing here?"

"I thought you'd never ask," I said gravely. "Did you know a Bob Summers down here?"

His expression changed again. "You mean the Bob Summers who was the night watchman at a building down the street from here?"

"That's the one."

"I knew him. What about it?"

"Did he have any family?"

He let his breath out in a harsh sigh. "Yeah. He had a wife and two daughters and five grandchildren."

"Where do they live?"

"Why?" he asked roughly. "You want to sell them a nice beautiful casket or something like that?"

I shook my head. "I'm not in the selling line. I never could think of the right things to say."

"Then why do you want to know where they live?"

"Look," I said, "we've had a very interesting conversation, but you must admit that I don't know you very well. My reasons are my own business. If you and your friends are so curious, you can always follow me. That's your business."

He shook his head as if he'd been hit. "You're the craziest cat I ever met. Either you're a fool or you got more guts than anyone I know. What are you up to, man?"

"I'm up to finding out where Bob Summers's widow lives. If you don't want to tell me, someone else will."

He must have been holding his breath, for he suddenly let it out in a big sigh. "Okay," he said. He paused only a moment longer. "Walk down this way one block, then go two blocks to the right. You'll see an old, beat-up, dirty-gray house that looks as if it would collapse any minute. Mrs. Summers and her two daughters and her five grandchildren live in three rooms on the top floor."

"Where are the fathers of the grandchildren?"

"One of them," he said bitterly, "was killed in Vietnam. The other was killed in a civil rights march in Georgia. Any other questions?"

"No." I finished my drink. "I'll see you around, George."

"I doubt it." He looked at me fiercely. "You don't know what you're walking into, man. What do you think the odds are of you coming out of it?"

"I don't know. What are they?"

"Maybe a hundred to one. Maybe more."

I pulled a dollar from my pocket and put it on the bar. "I'll take some of the action. Where do I go to make the bet?"

He shook his head again. "You just, don't know, man."

"I know," I said. "Look, baby, I've been around a long time and I expect to be around much longer. I'm not pushing anyone and I don't intend to be pushed. You can listen in on everything I have to say to anyone. This isn't any Mickey Mouse game to me either. It's for real. I'll still see you." I got up and walked out. I went down the street, following his directions without looking back.

The house was gray with fatigue and bent with age. I climbed the stairs, expecting them to collapse any minute, aware that there were probably a hundred eyes following me. When I reached the top, I knocked on the door.

Faint sounds drifted through the wood—the shuffling of feet, muted voices, and once the shrill voice of a child. Finally the door opened a few inches and the face of a woman looked out. It was a black face lined with the record of untold sorrows and frustrations. There was nothing but hostility in her eyes.

"What do you want, white man?" she asked.

"Are you Mrs. Summers?" I replied.

"I'm the Widow Summers." Her voice was flat, as though to tell me that I was barred from seeing any of her grief.

"I'm from an insurance company in New York," I said. "We carried the insurance on the Belters Building where your husband worked. While we don't have any insurance on him, we do feel a certain responsibility. I think there'll be some more later, but in the meantime I want to give you this."

I took out two hundred dollars and thrust it toward the door.

"What's that for?" she asked, making no move to take it.

"For whatever you want to do with it."

"I ain't taking no charity."

"Who the hell said anything about charity?" I said angrily. "If you're too damn stiff-necked to spend it where it needs to be spent, then give it to your grandchildren to play with. Maybe they'll be smarter about it than you are." I pushed the money into her hand and turned and went down the stairs.

I passed a number of men on my way back to the car.

I thought I recognized a couple of them as having been in the bar, but I paid no attention. I had almost reached my car when I noticed another one parked in front of me. There were two men sitting in it. Both of them were white. As I neared them, they got out to stand casually on the sidewalk. Neither of them looked at me until I reached them.

"Looking for something, Mac?" one of them asked me. I stopped and studied them. They looked like twins, and twin to dozens of other men all over the country. They had the same expressionless faces, the same flat stare that looked through a person and dismissed him. I didn't have to look any further to know that there was a bulge under the left armpit of each one. I knew their breed and I wondered what they were doing here.

"No," I said. "Just taking a little walk. Recommended by my doctor as healthy."

"Yeah. It's a good idea, Mac. If you want to be healthy, you'll just keep on walking."

"Sure," said the second one. "Just walk west until you're about a mile on the other side of the beach. Then take a deep breath." He snickered in appreciation of his own wit.

"Thank you," I said gravely. "I'll remember that." I started to move around them.

"Hey, just a minute," the first one said. "I still want to know what you're doing down here."

"That," I said evenly, "is my business."

"We could make it our business."

"You wouldn't like it. The pay is too small."

"A smart ass," one of them said. "Maybe we'd better teach him something."

"Yeah," the other said.

They moved slowly toward me, separating so that I would be between them.

TWO

Time was moving like a river of sorghum molasses. I was wishing I'd brought my gun with me from the hotel. So far the two men hadn't made a move to go for their guns, but it looked as if they at least intended to beat me up. The reason was baffling. The only thing I could think of was that they may have thought I was following them for some reason. In the meantime, I was concentrating on trying to watch both of them. I didn't see or hear the car that pulled up. I guess they didn't either.

"What's going on here?" a voice demanded.

The three of us looked up at the same time. It was a black-and-white police cruiser with two cops in it.

"Nothing at all, officer," one of the two men said. "We just spotted an old friend and got out of the car to say hello to him."

"Well, break it up anyway," the cop said. "There's to be no congregating on the streets, black or white."

I was already in motion, walking quickly toward my car. I was in it by the time the cruiser started to pull away. I started the motor, made a fast U-turn, and was leaving before the two men had climbed back into their car. I kept glancing into the rearview mirror, but I didn't see any signs of them following me. I drove north to Sunset and then went up it until I had reached the Scandia restaurant. It was time for lunch.

An attendant took my car and I went inside. I had a couple of dry martinis and ordered lunch. I kept thinking about the two men, but nothing about their attempted attack made any sense. I had never seen them before. There was no way they could have known I was an insurance investigator. Even if they did know, why try to question me and threaten to beat me up? Unless they thought I was somebody else.

After lunch I looked up Belters, Inc., in the phone book. The main office was on Wilshire Boulevard not far from where I was. I drove over. It was a new building. Belters had one whole floor and part of another. I went upstairs.

I stepped out of the elevator into an elegant reception room. The most elegant thing in it was the girl behind the desk. I've often thought there was a relationship between the beauty of a receptionist and the success of the company. If that is true, Belters must have been coining money.

"Yes, sir?" she said as I approached her desk.

"I'd like to see Mr. Frank Jeffers. My name is Milo March."

"What is it in reference to, Mr. March?"

"I represent your insurance company, the New York Office."

"Just a minute, Mr. March." She picked up the phone and dialed three numbers. She repeated the information I had given her, listened, and hung up.

"Mr. Jeffers's secretary will be right out."

I thanked her and moved to a chair from which I could appreciate her. It wasn't long until a door opened and another girl entered. She was equally breathtaking.

"Mr. March?" she asked. It was pretty silly since I was the only man in the room.

I nodded and stood up.

"Come this way," she said. "Mr. Jeffers will see you now."

I followed her past a stable of typists and several offices. It was a nice view from where I was. That secretary had more movements than a rare watch.

She finally stopped in front of a door, tapped on it gently, and then opened it. "Mr. March is here," she said.

"Send him right in," a voice called.

She stepped to one side and I walked in. It was a large office, expensively furnished. The man behind the desk was small and slender, with a sharp face and an air of being all tensed up and ready to go. I had a feeling that he was always like that. He jumped to his feet and held out his hand.

"Glad to see you, Mr. March," he said. We shook hands and he indicated the chair beside his desk. "How long have you been in the city?"

"I got in last evening."

"And you're with Intercontinental?"

"Yes."

"I hope you'll pardon me, Mr. March, but may I see any identification you have showing that you're with the company?"

I nodded and dug out my Intercontinental card and passed it over to him. He studied it before giving it back.

"I'm sorry to ask for that, but I assume that you will want to talk about certain matters involving the corporation and I felt I had to be certain."

"That's all right," I said. "As you probably know, we carried the insurance on your building in southeast Los Angeles and on the lives of Mr. Masters and Mr. Beld. There seems to be some belief that they both died in the fire."

"A terrible thing," he said, shaking his head. "And I can assure you, Mr. March, that it is more than a belief. Mr. Masters and Mr. Beld were there working that night. I myself spoke to Mr. Masters on the phone shortly before the violence started. I had been listening to the news on television and urged him to leave at once, but he just laughed at me. Yes, it's a tragic thing."

"I'm sure you all feel that way," I said. "I suppose, however, that you are aware there has been no positive identification of the three bodies found in the rubble and that there will probably never be such identification."

"Does that mean your company is going to refuse to pay on those policies?" He sounded angry.

"Not necessarily. It will probably mean some delay and could mean a delay of seven years. What actually happens will depend to a large degree on the report I will eventually write. I was fully expecting that you and the others would be glad to cooperate."

"We will," he said. "But how? On what?"

"I want to learn as much about the two men as I can—their habits, their financial condition, also information about the corporation."

"That's all?" he asked bitterly. "Do you mean they may refuse to pay on the building insurance?"

"I doubt it, but this kind of investigation is necessary. When a case is settled, our files must contain all possible information pertaining to the reasons for a payment of the face value of a policy. This is important for many reasons, but especially in providing our actuaries with the information they need to estimate future premiums. In a way, I imagine that you keep similar information in your files."

"Yes, I suppose we do," he said reluctantly. I had him shook up—which was the way I wanted him. "What can I do to help?" he asked.

"I'm sure that your knowledge of the business is probably greater than anyone else's, so I'll go over those points with you. In addition, you must have known both men quite well and can help there, too. How long have you been with the corporation?"

"Twenty years."

"You probably possess more information than you think. By the way, wasn't it rather odd for Mr. Masters to keep a large office in the Belters Building downtown when I'm sure he had a very adequate suite of offices here?"

"It might be unusual for some men, but it wasn't for Mr. Masters. We own about ten office buildings, including this one, and Mr. Masters had offices in each one of them."

"Why?"

"He was extremely active in every phase of our business. Although we're quite large now, you could almost say it was a one-man business. He kept duplicate records of all our dealings in every office, so that wherever he was, he could look up anything he needed at once."

"There was help in all of the offices?"

"Yes, usually two girls. We had two colored girls in the office that burned up. It was quite unfair of the rioters to burn that building."

"Sure," I said. "Why was he down there that night?"

"He was having a meeting with Mr. Beld. As you may know, Mr. Beld operated the television store on the ground floor. I believe they were going over the inventory and they were also making plans to open similar stores in other parts of Los Angeles."

"Mr. Masters even bothered to check inventories himself?"

Jeffers nodded. "He was extremely active in every aspect of our business. That covers quite a number of different activities. Nothing was too small for his attention."

"If," I said, "Mr. Masters is dead, who is going to do that for the corporation in the future?"

"We'll carry on," he said confidently. "Actually we have very fine and able people here. It's true that they haven't taken the completely active part they might have liked, but they're all capable. We'll continue in the tradition."

I almost expected him to get up and wave a flag.

"By the way, what is the condition of the corporation?"

"In what way?" He sounded puzzled.

"Financially."

"Oh! Sound. Very sound."

"What would you say is the present value of the holdings?"

"Offhand, I'd say between thirty and forty million dollars. And we're growing every year."

"How about your cash reserves?"

He looked nervous again. "They're never very high. Mr. Masters believed in reinvesting as fast as possible. It's always worked very well."

"But how high? How much do you have in the bank right now for general expenses?"

"I don't know the exact amount, but it's around a half million dollars."

"Isn't that pretty low for a business this size?"

"It's always been quite adequate."

"Who signed the checks?"

"Mr. Masters and myself. Two signatures were always needed."

"Only one bank account?"

"Oh, no. There are four separate accounts. The half million figure is the total of all four accounts."

"That's all?"

"Yes—except for one other small account."

"Tell me about it," I said.

"Well, it's a special account. Only one signature is required on it—Mr. Masters's. It has always been a special expense account to be used by Mr. Masters in the pursuit of new ventures, that sort of thing."

"How much is in it?"

"It usually ranges from twenty-five to a hundred thousand dollars. Whenever it drops to twenty-five thousand, we make a deposit from one of the other accounts."

"Interesting," I said. "I'd like to know within the next day or two the present amount in that account. I'd also like to know when the last deposit was made in the account and the amount. And I'd like to know if there have been any large withdrawals. If so, when? Now, what was Mr. Masters's salary as president?"

"One hundred thousand a year. Plus bonuses at the end of the year, which were voted by the board of directors."

"I presume he had a personal bank account?"

"Yes, sir."

"Did you have anything to do with keeping the records on that account?"

"No, sir."

"You don't know how much money he kept there?"

"No."

"Did Mr. Masters have any bad habits?"

"No, sir. So far as I know, he never took a drink or smoked a cigarette."

"I don't consider drinking a bad habit," I said indignantly. "What about broads? Not that I consider them a bad habit either."

"Broads?" By now Jeffers was very nervous.

"Like in females. Did he chase them?"

He cleared his throat and tugged at his collar. "Mr. Masters did not take me into his confidence."

"I didn't ask you that. I asked you if he chased broads. Don't be coy, Jeffers. I can and will ask all over town. If he chased broads, somebody will tell me."

He cleared his throat again. "As I said, Mr. Masters did not confide in me, but I believe that he and Mrs. Masters had not had a close relationship the last several years and that he did occasionally become interested in young ladies."

"Well phrased, Jeffers," I said dryly. "Did the young ladies drift in and out one at a time, or was he given to being interested in several at the same time?"

"I—I believe he was sometimes interested in more than one at a time."

"Active old boy, wasn't he? Any idea of what that little hobby cost him?"

"No. If he spent any money on the young ladies, I would presume it came out of his personal account."

"Know who any of the young ladies were?"

"No, sir."

I had a feeling he was lying, but I let it go for the time being. "Did Mr. Masters like to gamble?"

He seemed relieved to get away from the women. "He enjoyed it occasionally, but it wasn't a regular thing. Once in a great while he would take three or four days off and go to Reno. But I don't believe he ever bet any large sums."

"That was considerate of him." I glanced at my watch. "Well, Mr. Jeffers, I expect I've taken up enough of your time for today. I don't want to interfere with the well-oiled machinery. But I'll be back tomorrow morning and we'll go into a few other aspects of the business."

"I shall do my best to help you, Mr. March," he said stiffly.

I had an idea he was holding himself together by sheer force and would collapse as soon as I was gone. Then he'd worry most of the night and be good and ripe in the morning.

I nodded to him and walked out. I was about to head for the elevators when I had a sudden idea. I stopped beside a desk and waited until the girl looked up at me. "Could you tell me if there's a Miss Kitty Harris working here?"

The girl nodded. "Executive secretary, whatever that means. That's her office back there." She pointed to a door at the rear of the room.

I went over and knocked lightly.

"Come in," a voice called.

I opened the door and stepped inside. It was a small office. The girl sitting behind the desk was pretty and stacked like the well-known brick building. She had long, beautiful red hair. She was probably between thirty and thirty-five. The only thing to mar her beauty was a few bitter lines in her face.

"When you're through taking an inventory," she said, "you might tell me who you are and what you want."

"Sorry," I said. "I always get overcome in the presence of beauty. I'm Milo March. I work for Intercontinental Insurance. We carried policies on the building that was burned downtown and on the two men from here who were killed in the fire. I wondered if I could talk to you for a few minutes."

"Why not? I wasn't doing anything but drawing pictures in my shorthand book. I get a good salary for that—although I'll probably be fired in the next few days—as soon as somebody realizes I'm still here. Sit down."

I took the chair next to her desk. "Did you know Harry Masters?"

She gave me a wry smile. "I knew him."

"Were you a friend of his?"

"Friend, hell. I was his mistress—one of them."

"What kind of a man was he?"

"Do you mean in bed or out of it? Either place he was a ring-tailed son of a bitch. In bed, he thought he was the answer to a woman's prayers. He'd give you a quick jump—and I do mean quick—then pat you on the rear end and tell you how great he'd been. But aside from those little things, he was a generous man."

"Is that how you got nineteen percent of the corporation stock?"

"Yeah. I bought it by staring at the ceiling. I got this job the same way. Does that shock you?"

"I haven't been shocked since I was eight years old and learned that storks didn't do anything but stand around on one leg or build nests in chimneys. ... Are you on the board of directors?"

"I'm supposed to be, but I was never notified of any meetings."

"Do you know anything about the condition of the company?"

"No. And I don't care as long as that stock pays dividends. They can fire me, but they can't take the stock away from me. ... Hey, are you thinking that Harry swung with some of the loot?"

"Do you think he did?"

"I never thought about it," she said. "I guess he would have been capable of it. If he did, I guess he didn't get very far with it. I hated to think of him dying that way."

"When did you break up with him?"

Her lips twisted in what was meant to be a smile. "I guess I never did. Harry hated to let go of anything, even when he didn't have any use for it. He's been showing up at my place about once a month for a quickie, and then he'd take off. Sometimes I was surprised that he even bothered to take his hat off."

"All right," I said. "I'll leave now, but I may want to come back and talk to you again. Thank you, Miss Harris."

"Call me Kitty. Everyone else does. And you know what that's a pet name for. Come around anytime. If I'm no longer employed here, the personnel department will give you my address—although, come to think of it, it's in the phone book, too."

"I'll see you," I promised her.

I opened the door and went straight to the elevator. Downstairs I checked the time. It was still early in the afternoon, but I decided I had done enough work for the day. I drove back to the hotel.

I bought a paper and went up to my room and ordered a bucket of ice. When it came, I had a refreshing drink of V.O. while I read the paper. I undressed and made another drink. Then, stretched out on the bed with my drink in one hand, I thought about the day. I was fairly well pleased with it. I hated to admit it, but Martin Raymond had been right about one thing. There was a feeling about the case. Something was wrong. Maybe Masters had died in a fire started by rioters; maybe he hadn't. There was still something that didn't smell right.

I finished the drink and a cigarette and took a nap. I still hadn't adjusted to the change in time.

It was six o'clock when I awakened. I took a quick shower and dressed in some California-type clothes. Downstairs I checked on messages. There weren't any.

I got the Cadillac and drove down to the Casa Del Monte in Hollywood. It was the cocktail hour and the place was almost full. The only empty stool was at the end of the bar next to a lovely blonde. It was the only place I would have taken if there had been no one else in the bar. Bo spotted me and came over. He was carrying a ledger book. He put it and a pencil down in front of me. "Sign your name in it," he said.

"Why?" I asked.

He laughed. "It's the membership list of a private club here. Sign it, give me a dollar, and during certain hours—such as right now—you get a double drink for the price of one."

"Gimmicks," I said. "Will you send me my double drinks when I go back to New York?"

"Sure. Just sign it."

I opened the book and signed my name. Then I put a dollar on the bar. He took the money and gave me a small numbered card.

"Now that we're through with the nonsense," I said, "may I have a double dry martini? And give the young lady a double of whatever she's drinking."

"Sure," he said. "Incidentally, Melody, this is Milo March, my father. Father, this is Melody."

"Oh," I groaned. "We're starting that jazz again. If I had been your father, I'd have drowned you when you were a pup. ... Hello, Melody."

"Hello, Milo," she said. "Or should I call you Father, too?"

"I've beaten broads to a pulp for less than that. Say, bar boy, where are the drinks?"

"Coming up," he said. He danced away and was soon back with a double martini and what looked like a double screwdriver.

"Is there booze in that?" I asked the girl.

"There'd better be," she said, "or it'll be a stormy night."

"Your girl?" I asked Bo.

"She says she is," he replied. "So far I haven't been able to talk her out of it."

"This isn't my day," I said. "I come in here, a lonely stranger, and there's only one empty stool. It's next to the only beautiful girl in the joint, so I think I'm throwing nothing but sevens. Then it turns out that she goes along with the house. Now, if I make a pass, I'll get a mickey. If I don't, she'll think I'm a boob who doesn't know a pretty girl when he sees one."

They both laughed and Bo went off to wait on other customers. I worked on my martini and talked with Melody. She was all right. I decided that maybe Bo was growing up. Then I got a shock. I glanced down at the end of the bar and there was one of the two men I had encountered downtown that morning.

I finished my drink without talking much, and motioned for Bo. "Two more," I said when he arrived.

He brought the drinks, and I put my money on the bar, but kept my hand on it. "Don't make it too obvious that you're looking," I said, "but there's a guy down at the other end of the bar. He's fairly small, hatchet-faced, and he didn't buy his clothes on Madison Avenue. See if you know him."

He nodded and went to the cash register to ring up my money. When he came back with the change, he said, "I don't know his name, but he's a hood. I was told that he'll do anything for the bread—even to taking a contract. I've noticed he always carries a piece."

"Does he live around here?"

"Probably. He comes in once or twice a week, sometimes

with another guy who looks like him. I don't know his name either, but I was tipped off about him by another customer."

"Okay. I just wondered."

"What's the scene?" he asked.

"I'll tell you later. How late are you working tonight?"

"Another hour," he said. "Why?"

"You and Melody want to have dinner with me?"

"Sure." He laughed. "As long as it's on the expense account."

"I'll call New York and ask them," I said gravely. "Okay, whenever your relief shows."

He nodded and went back to work. Melody and I talked—mostly about music, about which I know very little, and some about girls, about which I know a lot. We had just finished our second doubles when Bo came around from behind the bar.

"All set," I said. "Let's go."

I slid off the stool and the three of us walked out. I didn't look back. I had parked the Cadillac near the side of the building. I led them to it and we got in.

"Whatever you do," Melody said, "it must be a nice business. I know it's a nice car."

"He's fuzz," Bo said.

"Really?" she asked me.

"Some people consider me fuzz," I answered, "but they're all idiots. And fuzz don't consider me fuzz. Where can we go and have a nice quiet dinner?"

"There are some good places out in the Valley," Bo said.

"Okay. We go to the Valley. And don't anybody talk until I tell you it's all right."

I made a U-turn, hit Hollywood Boulevard, and headed

west. The entrance to the freeway was two blocks away. I kept my eyes on the rearview mirror half the time. When I turned into the freeway, I jumped the Cadillac to sixty-five miles an hour. Nobody followed me from the Boulevard to the freeway. I relaxed a little, but I still kept looking in the mirror every few minutes.

"All right," I said, "tell me when we turn off this thing."

I kept watching the rear, especially when we took the off ramp. No one followed me, so I eased up some as I followed instructions on how to reach the restaurant.

"Expecting someone to follow you?" Bo asked.

"Just being careful," I said. "It keeps my insurance premiums lower."

We found the restaurant and had a good dinner. Then I drove them home.

"Find out that guy's name for me," I told Bo as we said good night. He said he would.

Back at the hotel, I picked up a paper. I had a couple of nightcap drinks while I read the paper and watched the late news on TV. Then I went to sleep.

After breakfast the next morning, I got in the car and headed directly for the Belters office on Wilshire. I parked back of the building and went up to the offices. The same receptionist was there.

"Mr. March to see Mr. Jeffers," I said.

She smiled and reached for the phone. She passed on the message before giving me another smile. "Go right in, Mr. March."

I went through the door and Jeffers's secretary was waiting

for me. Again she escorted me back to his office. He looked as if he hadn't slept too well, but he made an effort to be bright and alert.

"Good morning, Mr. March," he said. "Glad to see you are in early."

"The early bird catches something," I said. "I can never remember whether it's a worm or a cold." I sat down without waiting to be invited and lit a cigarette. This is known as psychological warfare. It works. I noticed that his hands were shaking slightly as he shuffled the papers on his desk.

"I realize," I said, "that you are very busy—especially at this time—so I'll try not to take up too much of your time. Did you find out about that special account?"

"Yes. I checked it as soon as you'd left. There was a fairly large withdrawal about ten days ago. It was not, however, an unusual transaction. Mr. Masters quite often took a large amount of cash with him when he went on a business trip. That way, if he ran into something that looked good for us, he could take an option on the property and pay for it in cash. If it didn't work out, he would then put the money back into the account."

"He went on a business trip about ten days ago?"

"He must have. He didn't tell me—but then he never did. I knew he was gone for three days. Eventually, if it hadn't been for the fire, he would have turned in a report and an expense voucher. Since he didn't replace the money, he must have made some sort of deal. The papers were probably in his pocket. But I'm sure that we will receive some confirmation soon from the other party."

"Sure," I said cynically. "How large was the withdrawal he made ten days ago?"

"Seventy-five thousand dollars," Jeffers said reluctantly. "As I just told you, that was not especially unusual. And he always accounted for all of the money he took on such a trip."

"Yeah, but now it's hard to communicate with him. Do you suppose he told anyone where he was going?"

"I really don't know. He may have told his secretary or his wife."

"Who is his secretary?"

"Miss Lester. She occupies a small office next to his."

"Did he play footsie with her, too?"

"I really don't know," he said stiffly.

"Okay," I said. "So much for the seventy-five big ones. There are a number of other things that excite my curiosity. All the stockholders are members of the board of directors?"

"Yes."

"What does that mean?"

"Not much," he admitted. "Not too many of them show up for meetings. Mr.

Masters made all the decisions himself. The board's approval was a mere formality."

"I had a feeling about that. What about his wife? Did she attend the meetings?"

"I believe she came down once."

"What about you?"

"I was at most meetings. I believe I've missed two since I've been here."

"I notice that you own five percent of the stock. Did you purchase that or was it given to you?"

"It was given to me as a bonus one year when business was especially good."

"I'm glad to hear that Masters was so considerate of his employees. How about Miss Harris? I believe she holds nineteen percent of the stock."

He was getting nervous again. "That is correct."

"Has she been here long enough to receive that much stock as a bonus?"

"Miss Harris has worked here approximately three years, but it's possible that she purchased the stock. I wouldn't know."

"And Mr. Beld, the brother-in-law—was he active in the corporation?"

"No. He ran the store in the building that was burned, but that was the extent of his activity. I imagine that Mr. Masters gave the stock to Mr. Beld only because he was his wife's brother."

"Very generous," I murmured. "Now we come to the most interesting stockholder of all. Fascinating is probably a better word." I stopped and stared at him. He was beginning to sweat. "I refer to Miss—I presume it is Miss—Sherry LaSalle. A romantic name. I notice that she owns fifty-one percent of the stock. A nice round number. How long has she been in this enviable position?"

"About two years."

"And I suppose that she also received her shares of stock for ... services rendered?"

"I wouldn't know the details," he said faintly, "but I believe she made an investment in the corporation about that time. Mr. Masters held a proxy on her voting stock."

"Shrewd," I said. "Both of them. Does Miss LaSalle have an occupation other than owning stock?"

"I believe she's a dancer."

"A fine occupation. Good salaries. I imagine she has excellent assets. Do you happen to know where she works?"

"I believe in nightclubs, but I don't know for sure."

"Do you know where she can be reached?"

"No, but I imagine she's listed in the Los Angeles telephone directory."

"An excellent suggestion. I would never have thought of it myself. Incidentally, has she been in touch with the office since the unfortunate accident?"

"I—I don't believe so."

"Overcome by grief," I said sympathetically. I can be a bastard when I have to. "Tell me something else, Mr. Jeffers. If Mr. Masters is really dead, who will make the far-flung empire of Belters function?"

"Why, I imagine all of us."

"But somebody has to say yes and no. Won't that person be Miss LaSalle since the proxies are worthless once Mr. Masters is no longer among us?"

"I never really thought about it. ... I suppose you're right."

"Is it your impression that Miss LaSalle is a shrewd businesswoman?"

"I really don't know. I've never even met her."

"Makes for an interesting business relationship, doesn't it?

Well, Jeffers, I wish you luck. If I need any more information from you, I'll be in touch."

I stood up and shook hands with him. His hand was just a little clammy. I took two steps toward the door and turned back. "Can you think of any reason why Mr. Masters would like people to think he was dead if he is actually alive?"

He fell apart again and tried to hide his shaking hands among the papers on his desk. "Good heavens, no. What are you suggesting, Mr. March?"

"I wasn't suggesting anything. I just asked a question. I'll see you around—I hope."

I left his office. His secretary was hovering outside as though she knew he was of troubled mind.

"Where do I find Miss Lester?" I asked her.

"Right down there," she said, pointing. "Next to the door with Mr. Masters's name on it." She glanced at Jeffers's door. "Is—is he all right?"

"Sure. He's just having a slight attack of vapors, but he'll recover. If you have anything stronger than ice water in the place, give him a shot and he'll be as good as new—well, as good as he was before."

She glared at me. For a minute I thought she was going to do something melodramatic, like calling me a beast, but she settled for the glare.

I went on to the office she had pointed out and knocked gently. A voice told me to come in.

This one was a blonde, about twenty-three, give or take a year. And pretty. And stacked. I was beginning to have a healthy respect for Masters's taste in women. A man who likes to be surrounded by pretty broads can't be all bad.

"Miss Lester?" I asked.

"Yes?" The question mark was obvious.

"My name is Milo March. I'm with Intercontinental Insurance. We carried the insurance on the Belters Building and on Mr. Masters and Mr. Beld."

"Oh! Come in, Mr. March."

I was already in, but I closed the door behind me and sat down on the only chair available. "I'll try not to take up too much of your time."

"That's all right. I haven't been very busy since ... the horrible accident."

"I can understand," I said. "I'm sorry to intrude at such a time, but I have to make a report. Have you worked here long?"

"Only a little more than a year."

"You were Mr. Masters's private secretary?"

"Yes."

"How did you get the job?"

"I was sent by an agency. Miss Harris had been promoted to executive secretary, and they needed someone to fill her old job. Mr. Masters interviewed me and hired me at once."

"I can see why," I said gently. "Pardon me for being blunt, but I'm a dirty old man and I like to clear certain things up right away. Did Mr. Masters ever make a pass at you?"

A faint smile brightened her face. "Oh, yes, the first week. And then almost every week after that. I can't imagine why he continued after I refused the first time."

"The name of the game is patience," I said. "I think Mr. Masters was a man who believed that if you shook a tree long enough, the apples would finally fall. What did you do for Mr. Masters?"

"Private secretary. Took his letters and typed them. The same with memos. Answered the phone. Kept the files and saw that duplicates of everything were sent to the other offices. Made sure he had fresh water on his desk every morning. Also fresh flowers. Reminded him of people's birthdays. All the usual things."

"Was he out of town fairly often?"

"Yes. But usually for not more than two or three days. Even then he'd call me every day."

"Did you have anything to do with taking care of his personal bank account?"

"Oh, no."

"About ten days ago he took a trip. You were here then?"

"Yes. I phoned for the reservations and picked up the airline tickets for him."

"Tickets? Plural?"

"Two tickets." She smiled. "I guess he found someone who didn't say no to him. I was glad, because I've often thought he was very lonely."

"I don't think he ever stayed lonely for long," I said dryly. "Where did he go on this last trip?"

"Reno, Nevada."

"Do you know what kind of business he expected to do there?"

"I didn't get the feeling he was going on business. I thought he just wanted to get away for a few days, maybe gamble a little."

"He liked to gamble?"

"Oh, yes. I remember he said he found it relaxing. He used to go to Reno or Las Vegas about once a month. He was always bringing back souvenirs for me—matchbooks and chips from the casinos."

"Did he lose much?"

"I don't think so. He usually said he won. I don't think he bet a lot of money. He just played for fun."

"That's Vegas and Reno," I said, "just fun places. Do you know where he played up there?"

"I remember Harrah's and something called Cal Neva. I don't know where else. Oh, yes. There was another place, but I don't know whether it was a gambling casino or not. One time after he'd returned, a bar bill came from Reno. It was from a place called The Sewer. I gave it to him and that's all I know about it."

"A bar bill? I thought he didn't drink."

"I don't think he did around here, but I'm sure he did when he went away for a few days. He never told me anything about it. I know that there were a lot of bar bills on his credit cards. I never asked about them and he never told me."

"Smart," I said. "Did you get all of the bills on his credit cards?"

She nodded.

"What about from stores?"

"Yes."

"Were there many things such as women's clothes, perfumes—that sort of thing on the bills?"

"A lot of bills were from shops that catered to women."

"Was there anything recently about his actions that would make you think that he was maybe nervous or planning on taking a long trip?"

"No, I don't think so. I'm sure that I would have noticed it if there had been anything of that sort."

"Okay," I said. "Let's try something else. You were pretty close to him during the hours he spent here at the office. Can you remember anything that happened recently that was unusual? Something you didn't expect?"

She thought for a minute, then nodded. "There was one thing right after he came back from Reno. It was very strange. The phone rang and the receptionist said that there was a Mr. Benetto here to see Mr. Masters. I told him, and he got a funny look on his face and said to have Benetto come in. I told the receptionist, and a moment later two men walked into the office. They were both small men, dressed in expensive but funny-looking suits. I hate to sound dramatic, but the only thing I could think about was that they looked sinister. Mr. Masters asked me to leave the office. Later, after they were gone, he said something about them handling some charity donations for him."

"Interesting," I said. "Well, I won't bother you anymore now. I may be back to see you another time. Thanks, for now."

"You're welcome," she said. "I don't know whether I'll be here or not. Nobody knows what's going to happen. Some of the girls think that everyone will be fired."

"I'll find you through personnel," I said.

I left and went downstairs to where the car was parked. I leaned against it and thought about the morning's efforts. The more I heard about Mr. Masters, the more I was certain there was something wrong. And the two little men interested me the most. Her description of them sounded very much like the two I had met the day before.

"Hello, Whitey," a voice said.

I looked around. It was the young black man I had met the day before. He was walking across the parking lot toward me.

THREE

This was the man named George Carver Henderson. He had been alternately hostile and friendly when I'd met him in the bar. I wondered which he was now. And how had he found me? Then I decided I was getting too jumpy. I relaxed and waited for him to come up to me.

"Hello, Brownie," I said when he was a few feet away.

He laughed. "Still a cool cat," he said. "Man, I've been waiting an hour for you."

"I'm flattered," I said. "Just two questions. Why and how?"

"I'll answer the how first. You told me your name, but you didn't tell me where you were staying. I was going to start phoning hotels, but I figured that would be a bad scene. You'd told Mrs. Summers that you were from the insurance company that covered the Belters Building. So I figured out you'd be nosing around the main office, and I came up here. I spotted the heap and the rest was just waiting."

"And the why?" I asked.

"There's a little more to that. Besides, I want to talk to you some more first. You're a curious cat and I want to know what makes you purr."

I laughed. "The same thing that makes any tomcat purr. I have to visit some other places. Want to ride along?"

"Why not? It's a groovy heap and I got nothing else to do."

I got behind the wheel and he slipped in next to me. As I drove out on Wilshire, turning north on the next street, I glanced at my watch. "It's not far from noon. I think we'll stop at a watering hole, have something to drink, and then some lunch."

"They allow spooks in there?" he asked with a grin.

"Sure. It's so dark they can't tell the difference. And if there's any problem, you can always buy some clown paint and go in white face."

"Man, you're too much. You sure you ain't passing?"

"I'm not sure of anything," I said.

I drove on until I reached Hollywood Boulevard, then turned down to my favorite bar. It was still a little bit before the lunch hour, so there weren't many people. Bo was working. We stopped at the bar and I ordered a martini. George ordered a bourbon and water.

"Bo," I said, "I want you to meet George Carver Henderson." They shook hands. "He was afraid you didn't serve spooks in here, so I brought him to see that's all you do serve. Some of them are black and some of them are white, and a few, early in the morning, are pale green, but they're all spooks. Right?"

"Right," Bo said.

George laughed. "Crazy, man," he said, "just crazy."

"You got a better way to go?" I asked. "Come on. Let's drink these and switch to a table and some food."

We downed the drinks and went to a table. I ordered two more drinks and two steaks. When we'd finished them, I looked up some addresses in the phone book. We went out to the car and headed west. George wasn't talking, so I didn't volunteer to start.

I finally ended up in front of a fancy apartment building.

"I don't know how long I'll be inside, but wait in the car. I'll leave the keys in the ignition so you can turn on the radio."

"What's the matter?" he asked. "You afraid they wouldn't like it if I came in with you?"

"They'd probably rather see you than me. I'm going in on business, and I don't take anyone with me on business. Stop playing the hearts-and-flowers bit when there isn't any orchestra pit. Cool it, baby."

I heard him laugh as I got out, walked in, and rang the bell under the name of Masters. The door lock clicked. I entered and took the elevator to the third floor, pushed another button, and in a minute the door opened. The woman who looked out had probably once been very beautiful, but now her face was set in hardness and stamped with a network of wrinkles.

"Mrs. Masters?" I asked.

"I'm Mrs. Masters."

"My name is March and I'm with Intercontinental Insurance. We carried the insurance on your husband's business and on your husband and your brother. I'd like to talk to you for a few minutes."

"Come in," she said.

If the living room was any indication, it must've been a huge apartment—and expensive. She sat down in a large easy chair and I sat on the couch directly across from her.

"Does this mean that your company doesn't want to pay the insurance?" she asked.

"Not at all. It merely means that we make reports on every case. I'll admit that we're not very happy about the lack of positive identification, but it doesn't mean we're refusing to pay."

"You're unhappy," she exclaimed. "How do you think *I* feel? Maybe I buried the wrong man. That's what bothers me." She must have noticed some change in my expression. "You think that's odd? There's been nothing between Harry and me for fifteen years, and I was just as happy not to be bothered by him. He gave me all the money I wanted. I had my own interests, and he had his chippy-chasing. We got along better the past fifteen years than we ever did before."

"I can understand that," I said. "Do you feel certain that it was your husband in the building that night?"

"Of course. No one else would be that big a fool. Harry only lived for two things—girls and making money. If he wasn't out with a girl, then he'd be in one of the offices figuring out how to make more money."

"What about your brother?"

"He was a fool, too. He tried to hang on to Harry's coattails, but Harry would never let him grab anything. Larry kept trying, though. He never learned."

"Were you and your brother close?"

"Never."

"Did your brother have a family?"

"Neither chick nor child. He was always too busy with some wild scheme that was going to make him a million dollars, and he never made a dime until Harry let him run that television store."

"Did Mr. Masters leave you comfortably fixed?"

"Oh, yes. I have my own bank account and I've been putting money into it for the past fifteen years. Harry's conscience used to hurt him, and he would always give me quite a bit more than I needed to run the house. I'll get some insurance money, and I have ten percent of the corporation stock. I imagine I'll inherit another ten percent from Harry and whatever is in his personal bank account. Then I also have some property that I bought during the years."

She looked at me shrewdly. "As a matter of fact, Mr. March, I own this building. Harry never knew that he was paying rent to me." She laughed.

"Where did Mr. Masters have his bank account?"

"Security and Savings on Wilshire Boulevard."

She was being so calm about the whole thing that I decided I'd see if I could hit her between the eyes. "Do you think," I asked, "it might be possible Mr. Masters decided he wanted to cut out with some of his money and arranged for another body to be found in the fire?"

"How could he? He had no way of knowing those niggers were going to burn his building that night." She thought about it for a minute, then smiled. "You know that's the sort of thing Harry might've thought about. But you can be sure that he'd have to be certain he was taking most of the money and had already planned on what he was going to do with it. And he wouldn't have gambled on a chance like the building being burned by rioters."

"Maybe," I said. "Did you know he didn't own controlling interest in the corporation?"

"Of course I knew it. He couldn't help but brag all the time. He turned the control over to a chippy he got mixed up with a couple of years ago. She called herself a dancer, but all she did was take her clothes off while they played music. Harry had a proxy on all her shares. He explained it was some kind of tax dodge. You can be sure that Harry wanted the girl, but that he was too smart to give anything away."

"He liked to gamble, didn't he?"

"Yes. And I have to admit that he won most of the time. Harry was always very good at anything that had to do with money. I don't think he was ever very good in bed, but by the time he started to chase girls, he had enough money to make up for what he lacked between the sheets."

"Well, you've certainly been frank, Mrs. Masters."

"Why not?" she said with a shrug. "I've got enough money. Even if Harry pulled something like you suggested, I wouldn't care. And he'd get away with it. Harry was always smart."

"But you don't think he did anything like that?"

"No, I don't. First, it would involve depending on sheer luck. Harry was never much for that. Then, why should he do something like that? He could have just sold the business and walked away with millions. I wouldn't have tried to stop him. Neither would anyone else."

I had to admit that she had a point. It had been bothering me a little, but I still felt there was a smell to the case.

"Well, thank you, Mrs. Masters. I'm sorry I bothered you."

"Nonsense, young man. Stop again anytime. I like to sit down and talk. I even like to talk about Harry. He never did much for me except give me money, but I always kind of admired him. He was a no-good bastard—but he was good at it."

I thanked her again and left. George was still sitting in the car with the radio playing.

"Man," he said, "I was beginning to think you'd split and that any minute the fuzz was going to come along and accuse me of stealing the car."

"They wouldn't have bothered you," I said. "Everybody knows that all black people, even the ones on relief, drive Cadillacs. Now, me they're liable to stop on the grounds that I'm robbing you of your civil rights by driving this car."

He glanced at me as I pulled away from the curb. "I can't figure you out, man."

"Join the club. I can't figure myself out, and I've been working at it a lot longer than you have."

"Where are you going now?" he asked.

"To a bank. I'm going to see if I can float a small loan. I've been thinking about buying the *Queen Mary*. I feel the need for a yacht so I can get away from it all."

"Good idea. Where are you going?"

"I just thought I'd cruise between Long Beach and Santa Monica. Those big waves make me ill."

"You white folks got everything," he said. There was a smile in his eyes, if not on his face. "What about all these honkies you're going to see? They giving you a lot of sad stories about all them black people running around burning their property and killing their people? You tell them about all those white people who ran around for years burning our property and killing our people. You tell them it's still a one-sided score."

"I don't give them enough time for small talk." I glanced at him. "You feeling especially bloodthirsty today?"

"Not especially," he said. "If you're trying to ask where I stand, I'll tell you. I ain't a Black Power man or a Black Muslim man. I don't like violence, no matter where it comes from. I think Martin Luther King, Jr., was a great man. But you whites changed things. You passed a lot of laws and said, 'Hey, nigger, it says here that you can go to the same schools as we do, have the same kind of jobs, live in the same section of town.' Sure, it says that. But saying and doing is two different things. We got them on paper and that's all. So maybe it's time for a little violence. Sometimes it's the only answer. Like the white people who first came here. There came a time when they had to resort to violence to get what was coming to them. They won and so they became respectable. Maybe we'll win and become respectable."

"That was a pretty good speech. The next time I run for President, you can have second place on the ticket."

"You see," he said with a laugh, "you're still putting me down. Second place. Maybe I'll run for President and give you second place."

"I always thought I'd make a good *vice* president," I said as I turned into the parking place beside the bank. "I'll be right out. You can plan our campaign while I'm gone."

I went into the bank and asked to see the manager. I had to wait for a few minutes, and then I was sitting across a desk from a man who looked as if he knew everything about money. I introduced myself and showed him all of my identification.

He examined it carefully. "What can I do for you, Mr. March?" he asked.

"I'd like to get some information. I'm aware that you can give only limited data and that'll be fine. You have an account here in the name of Harry Masters. Did you know him?"

"Very well. He'd had an account here for years."

"You probably know that it is believed he died in a fire in the southeast section of town."

He nodded.

"My company," I said, "carried the insurance on the building that was burned and on the lives of Mr. Masters and his brother-in-law. That is why I'm looking for information."

"But, surely," he exclaimed, "there's no question about the validity of the insurance claims?"

"I didn't say there was. But we always make a careful check in cases such as this. We need the data for our files and the use of our actuaries. Sometimes it ends in a disputed claim; often it does not. Did Mr. Masters have an account here for any length of time?"

"About fifteen years."

"It was a personal account, wasn't it?"

"Yes."

"Can you give me some idea of the average balance?"

"I can't give you the exact figures, but it nearly always ran in six figures—the high six figures."

"Isn't that unusual for a checking account?"

"I suppose it is, but it wasn't for Mr. Masters. Quite often he'd draw a large sum which he used for business purposes, and then would replace it with a check drawn on his corporation."

"Can you tell me what the balance was when he died?"

"Yes. As a matter of fact it was quite low—in the low five figures."

"There was a large withdrawal just a few days before he died?"

"No," he said. "I had occasion to go through the records, as the executor is coming in tomorrow to go over everything. I was surprised to notice that Mr. Masters had been making large withdrawals, without replacing any of them, during the past month or so."

"Did Mr. Masters have a safe-deposit box here?"

"Strange you should ask," he said. "As a matter of fact, he did. Naturally we have no idea what he kept in it or what may be in it now. I couldn't help but notice that the executor became a little excited when I mentioned the state of the bank account. He asked about the safe-deposit box, too. All I could tell him was that Mr. Masters had been making trips to the box on the average of once a week until about two weeks before his death. Then he stopped."

"Who is the executor?"

"Mr. Robbins. He was Mr. Masters's attorney."

"Have you had other financial transactions with Mr. Masters?"

"Yes. One other. He recently bought some property, several buildings out in the Valley. He borrowed fifty thousand dollars from us to bind the deal, and when it was consummated we loaned him three and a half million dollars and took a mortgage for the entire amount. A short time later the responsibility for paying off the loan was transferred to the corporation."

"Isn't that an unusual way of doing business?"

"I suppose it is, but I understand that Mr. Masters quite often made such deals personally. His credit was good for it. Then he would transfer the business or property to the corporation."

"Well, thank you very much," I said.

I went outside. There was a phone booth in the parking lot. I looked up the number of Sherry LaSalle and dialed it. A sultry voice answered.

"Miss LaSalle?" I asked.

"Yes."

"My name is Milo March. I represent Intercontinental Insurance, which carried policies on the Belters Building that recently burned and on the late Mr. Masters and Mr. Beld. I'd like to talk to you if it's possible."

"Sure, honey. Anytime."

"How about today?"

"I couldn't make it today, honey. I just woke up and I have to have my breakfast and get ready to go to work tonight. Just a minute." There was a short silence while I waited. "I'll tell you what, honey. I'm working at The Bodies, a club up on the Strip. Why don't you come there tonight? Make a reservation and then I'll join you between numbers."

"All right," I said.

"See you, honey." She hung up.

I went back to the car and slid behind the wheel.

"Did we get the yacht?" he asked.

"Not yet. They want to make sure she's seaworthy, but it's only a formality." I drove out of the parking lot.

"Where we going now?"

"Downtown—to the bar where I met you yesterday."

"Uh-oh. You've already had enough integration for one day, huh?"

"No. I'm just tired of your company because you're the wrong sex."

"Maybe I'd better get Ruby to ride around with you. She's a swinging chick. I don't know how she feels now, but she used to dig you white cats. Some of our girls just don't have any class."

"I'll remember the offer," I said. "I'm through working until tonight. I feel like a drink and you said you wanted to talk to me. We can have a few and you can still talk if you want to."

"Man, it's going to ruin my image to be seen riding and walking around with a honky."

"Makes it even. You've been ruining your image with me right along."

"How's that?"

"Throwing out all that 'man' and 'cat' stuff. I'd guess you're pretty well educated. So you're putting up a smoke screen."

He laughed loudly. "I was born with a smoke screen. Besides, I'd guess you're pretty well educated too, but I don't hear you coming out with any Shakespeare."

"That's the way it goes. We start to do one thing and somehow it comes out differently. Take Marconi, for example."

"How'd you jump over to that cat?"

"Easy. He slaved over a hot soldering iron until he invented the little device that made him famous and a lot of other people rich. He probably thought he was going to turn on all those tubes and hear the voice of a Martian in outer space. What'd he get? Elvis Presley."

"For a minute I was afraid you were going to say Sammy Davis."

"He's all right, but I prefer Armstrong. I don't know what Edison set out to do, but he gets my nod because he made it possible for me to still buy a Bessie Smith record."

"You dig that stuff?"

"Yeah. Especially if it's New Orleans or Chicago."

He shook his head. "That's the disturbing thing about some of you honkies. Every once in a while, for no reason, you show some sense."

We had reached our destination, so I swung into a parking place in front of the bar without saying anything. We got out of the car and headed for the open bar door. "Ain't you going to lock the doors?" he asked.

"Why? If somebody wants to steal it, locking the doors won't stop him. Besides, I figure there'll be enough curiosity about me to give me temporary protection. Come on, I'll buy you a drink."

"Man you got more guts than brains." He shook his head and followed me inside.

There were only three men sitting at the far end of the bar. They looked up as George and I took stools near the doorway. I noticed George nod to them, and the bartender started for us at once. There was less feeling of hostility in the place than there had been yesterday. Instead, it seemed they had a sort of curious reserve as they looked at me.

"What'll you have, George?" the bartender asked as he came up.

"Bourbon and water."

The bartender looked at me. He didn't say anything, but he also didn't look quite as unfriendly as he had the day before.

"Bourbon with water backed," I said.

When he'd brought the drinks I put down a five-dollar bill. He took it and went away. I saw him hesitate at the cash register, then he pushed the keys and came back. This time I got change.

"Looks like I get fringe benefits by associating with you," I said as soon as the bartender was gone.

"Not that. You earned that yourself."

"How?"

"You ought to know. You're a smart cat. You earned that when you handed those two bills to Mrs. Summers."

"That don't mean anything. Lots of people toss a bone once in a while."

"Not that way. If you'd been tossing a bone, you would have come in here, made a big show of peeling off those two bills, and asked someone to see the Widow Summers got it. The Belters Corporation ain't done anything about her. You didn't make an announcement. You went up to see her yourself. The whole section knew it before you were off the street. I sometimes think we invented the grapevine. The whole street also knew about the two guys who were going to close in on you when you were leaving."

"I was going to ask if you knew them."

He shook his head. "They been hanging around since before the riots. We don't know them, but we know their kind. They're bad news."

"I can read that well," I said. "I just don't know why they're interested in me. It must be just my natural charm and good looks. ... You said you wanted to talk to me."

"Yeah," he said. He pulled on his drink. "What are you doing down here?"

"I told Mrs. Summers. I work for Intercontinental Insurance. We'd insured the building. We'd also insured the lives of the other two men who apparently died in the fire. I'm here to make a report."

"I don't dig it. Man, there was a riot down here. A lot of buildings were burned. A lot of people were hurt; a lot more arrested and beaten by the cops; and a few died. You going to find out which one of us black folks threw the torch into that building, send him up for it, and save your company a little money?"

"Almost three million dollars is not a little money. But that wouldn't save us the money anyway. We'd still have to pay the same even if I proved that you, say, set the building on fire and caused the death of the three men."

"Then what are you after?"

I lit a cigarette. "I know that black men and women and children set a lot of fires and did a lot of looting while the riots were on. You were probably right in the middle of it. I'm not even interested, except as part of what is happening in America. I haven't lost any black people and I'm not looking for any. You don't have a monopoly on Molotov cocktails. I think that fire was set by a white man. Who's going to pay special attention to one fire when a hundred have been set? Who's going to look for the ofay?"

He grinned. "You're old-fashioned, man. We don't call you an ofay anymore. You're a honky."

"I think I liked 'ofay' better. There was a certain kind of humor in its bitterness. It had a background, being descended in the tradition of the thieves' argot. It meant, at least for a time, that you could talk about your foe right in front of him without his knowing it. And it lacked the connecting link to a stereotype, a label, and a deliberate discrimination. 'Ofay' had a legitimate connection with the language of conceal-ment, as developed by thieves over several centuries; 'honky' has a legitimate connection with the language of hate and discrimination. Like 'hunkie' for all Hungarians at first, then finally for all Central Europeans who didn't speak such good English. And that's the end of my lecture for this semester. You'll get your degree in a plain, brown wrapper."

He was silent for a minute. "I guess you're right. I never thought about it much. So you mean that you think white men were responsible for that one fire, and you're trying to prove it. Why?"

"Remember, I'm riding a black Cadillac, not a white horse. And I get paid very well for it. Oh, I may enjoy it because there are certain people I don't like—and they come in all colors."

"Why would they do that?"

"There might be many reasons, but there are two good ones right on the surface. Somebody wanted money, or somebody wanted to get rid of one or two men. Maybe both."

"The two hoods?"

"They might have something to do with it. There may be

a link. On the other hand, they may have nothing to do with the case."

"I've something to say about that," he said. "I'll say it as soon as I get back from the men's room."

He walked to the back. I finished my drink and motioned to the bartender to give us two more.

When George came back, he stopped for a minute to speak to one of the men at the other end of the bar. Then he came to sit beside me.

"I think," he said carefully, "that I might feel the same way as you do about that case. I've told you I don't like violence, and that's certainly useless violence. But I have a special interest in you being right about what happened to that building and those men."

"What?"

"The explosion of black people down here had to happen. It was long overdue.

And some good may come out of it. But I think it would also help the whole picture if it turned out that one building was burned and three men killed for a useless reason by white men. By men who were completely numb to the rights of others and were conscious only of some gain for themselves."

I noticed that the man he had talked to was leaving the room, but I showed no awareness of it. "Well," I said, "we'll find out."

"You've sold me," he said. "If there's any help we—and I do mean we—can give you from here, you'll get it. We might be able to come up with something. The grapevine is pretty good."

"Thanks, George," I said. "I'll appreciate it."

The man who had left returned and went back to his drink at the end of the bar. I pretended not to be looking at him, but I saw him glance at George and nod his head.

"By the way," George said, "the two hoods are hanging around outside. They might have seen you come in here and be waiting for you."

"Probably," I said. I finished my drink. "I might as well be going. I've got to do a lot of work tonight and I want to get some rest."

"Want some of us to walk out with you?"

"I don't think it'll be necessary," I said. "So far they're not sure what I'm up to. If they become sure, they may lose interest in me, or they may decide to do something. But if I show up with an army now, they'll think that I'm afraid of them and they'll have to do something."

"Okay, but we'll be around."

"Thanks again. Incidentally, if you want to reach me I'm staying at the Continental Hotel. I'll be down, maybe tomorrow. If you can find out anything about the two guys, it'll be welcome. I'll see you."

"So long—Milo," he said.

I walked outside. I didn't look around, but out of the corner of my eye I glimpsed the two of them sitting in their car about a hundred yards behind me. I got into the Cadillac and drove off. Then I saw them pull away from the curb and follow. It seemed perfectly clear that they were interested in me and knew why they were interested. It was not just idle curiosity.

There were only two questions. Why were they interested, and when would they make their move? I had to guess the answers or the game would be over before it started.

FOUR

They certainly knew their business. They kept on my tail, without being obvious about it, all the way uptown, then north until I'd reached the hotel. I pulled in there, and as I turned the car over to an attendant, I saw that they had driven into the parking lot across the street. They were going to wait for me.

On the way in, I stopped at the desk. There was a message that Mr. Raymond had phoned from New York. Mr. Raymond could wait. I had intended to call him tomorrow morning and that's when I would do so. I went upstairs. It wasn't quite four o'clock, so I decided to rest for an hour. I took off my shoes and jacket and stretched out on the bed. I reached for the phone and asked the operator to call me at five o'clock. Then I went to sleep.

I was awakened by the sound of the phone. I picked up the receiver, thanked the operator, undressed, and took a fast shower. After I was dressed, I added one new piece of wearing apparel. I strapped on my shoulder holster, checked my .38, and slipped it into the holster. Then I put on my jacket and went downstairs.

While I waited for the attendant to bring my car, I looked across the street. They were still there, but one of them was already paying the parking ticket and they were ready to roll.

My car came and I pulled out of the hotel driveway and turned east on Sunset. I saw them drive out of the parking lot and fall in line three cars behind me. I smiled to myself and drove straight to the Casa Del Monte. I parked behind the stores across the street from the bar.

As I walked across to it, I saw that they had parked on Gramercy, where they could see my Cadillac. One of them would probably come into the bar and the other would stay outside. I went in and took a stool not far from the front door.

The cocktail hour was starting. The bar was fairly busy. Bo saw me and held up a martini glass. I nodded. He mixed one and came up and poured it.

"Melody enjoyed the dinner last night," he said.

"I'm glad she did. We should have gone somewhere afterwards, but I wanted to get up early this morning."

"I found out about that guy for you," he said.

"Good. He just came in and is going down to the other end of the bar. His last name is Benetto, isn't it?"

He nodded, surprised. "Gino Benetto. He works with a guy named Joe Cabacchi, also known as Joe Cabbage. They're both tough boys, in a lot of things. They deal in narcotics, broads, and stolen property, mostly business machines, TV sets, and radios—things like that. They both have connections with the Syndicate. They sometimes do jobs for them, especially on contracts. But they'll also take contracts from other people. Nice boys. I'll talk to you later." He went back to work.

I sipped my martini and idly watched the people at the bar, but didn't pay more than casual attention to Gino Benetto. He wasn't looking at me at all, which was a giveaway about his interest since he was looking at everyone else. I sipped my drink slowly because I didn't want to leave too soon. Finally I ordered a second one.

"Bo," I said, when he came with the fresh drink, "you ever hear of a place called The Bodies?"

"Sure. It's a joint up on Sunset. Great, if you go for strippers."

"Do they serve food there?"

"Yeah."

"Any good?"

"I don't know. I never ate there, but one of their bartenders used to come in here and he said you could get a great steak. I don't know if that meant the steak was the only good thing or merely that he was hung up on steak. Why?"

"I have to go there on business tonight. I was wondering whether to eat before or take a chance on them. Maybe I'll live dangerously."

"Some place to go on business. How are you going to keep your mind on what you're talking about?"

"Sheer will power," I told him with a smile.

"How's it going?" he asked.

"All right, I guess. I never know at this stage. I just go around asking questions and leaning on people a little, and it isn't long before they start unraveling."

"That's all there is to it? Maybe I ought to get in your racket. I notice you're wearing a little extra clothing tonight."

"Insurance policy," I said. "Anyone working for an insurance company has to carry some insurance or they'd think he was disloyal. Besides, there are some people getting curious about me—including our friend Benetto down there."

"Remind me to stay away from you," he said. He danced back down the bar to wait on a customer.

I sat and watched and listened, drinking slowly and enjoying it. The guy at the end of the bar got more nervous the longer I sat. I was beginning to enjoy myself. I got up and challenged the winner of the pool game that was going on. It was over in a few minutes. I won three games before someone beat me and I went back to serious drinking.

Bo came up with three martinis. "They're on the guys you beat."

"If that's the custom around here, you better give one to the guy who beat me. Who started this racket? You?"

He laughed. "Who else? Your little friend looks as if he's about to come apart at the seams."

"Yeah, he's not the patient kind."

I finished the three martinis, not gulping them, and decided it was time to leave. I said good night to Bo and walked slowly outside. I looked around for a minute, then ambled across the street to my car. I saw Benetto hurry out and join his pal in their car.

I backed the Cadillac out, but instead of heading for the street I drove the other way. There was a narrow one-way alley that ran down to Hollywood Boulevard between two buildings. As I entered it, I glanced back and saw them making a fast U-turn.

The alley was so narrow I had to drive slowly and then stop when I reached the sidewalk to make sure no one was going to step in front of me. I flicked on the turn signal to show that I was going to make a right turn and edged to the street, where I waited for a chance to get through the traffic. They were coming up the street. They must have spotted me. They saw the signal light and did what I had hoped they would. They wanted to be smart so that I would fall in behind them, then after a few blocks they'd let me pass them and just follow again. I saw an opening, changed my turn signal, shot through between cars, and headed in the opposite direction. I laughed as I thought of what they were saying.

I made a quick right turn on St. Andrews, drove one block, and turned left on Carleton Way. Another block and I turned left on Western. I was lucky and made the light at Hollywood. I shot through and up to Franklin, turned left and drove to Taft, then followed it back to Hollywood. A right turn and then I went down the ramp to the freeway. I got off at the next exit and stopped and parked at the first available place. They didn't show up, so I'd lost them.

Finally I drove down to the first street past Hollywood Boulevard and turned west. I stayed on it until I hit Highland, then went to Sunset Boulevard and straight up it. I found The Bodies without any trouble, parked, and went in.

"I believe I have a reservation," I told the man who greeted me. "My name is Milo March." I knew damn well I didn't have a reservation. I'd forgotten to phone them.

"Oh, yes," he said. "Miss LaSalle made it for you. She thought you might forget to phone."

"That was mighty nice of the little lady," I said, feeling like a Texan in town for a wild night. I followed him to a table that was going to be about as near to the show as was possible without having the dancers in my lap. A waiter showed up as soon as I hit the chair.

"How soon does the floor show start?" I asked.

"In about forty-five minutes, sir."

"Then bring me a double martini and a rare steak, extra rare. All I want with it is a salad with Roquefort dressing."

"Yes, sir," he said, and scuttled away.

I looked around. The place was a little more than half full, but it was early and they probably filled up later. The people looked like the ones in hundreds of similar clubs all over America. Many of the men were in little masculine groups, and the ones with women didn't look like they were with their wives. All of them gave the impression of being from out of town.

My martini came and I went to work on it. The steak followed soon afterwards. I cut it and took a bite. It was a good steak.

A small orchestra had appeared and was playing soft music. I finished my drink and turned to the steak and salad. Later I had a coffee. Then I just had time to get a drink, switching to bourbon on the rocks, when the orchestra hit a new note, a spotlight went on, and an emcee magically appeared. He introduced the first girl and vanished.

Altogether five girls appeared, one after another, and did their acts. Each one was supposed to have a specialty, but all it boiled down to was that they ended up wearing nothing except a G-string and pasties. In between they sang and

danced. It was a cinch that Julie Andrews and Barrie Chase*
had nothing to fear from them. Still, they received a lot of
applause, so I got the impression there weren't many music
lovers in the crowd.

Then the emcee came back and gave a big buildup before he
introduced Sherry LaSalle. She came on and I had to admit
that she was something else. To start with, she was beautiful—which I couldn't say about the others. She wasn't the
greatest in the voice department, but she could sing. When
she started stripping, I had to give her another high grade. The
girl had assets you don't find in a bank. I began to understand
why she had 51 percent of the Belting stock.

It didn't take me long to realize that she was doing a lot of
playing directly to my table. So she knew where I was sitting.
That was probably why she'd made the reservation for me.
She wanted to look over the audience before the real show
started.

She ended in the customary condition and took five or
six bows before the spotlight went out and the house lights
came up slightly. The orchestra went back to music that was
minus the grinds and bumps. I finished my drink and waited.
I didn't have to wait long. First I heard a faint sound sweep
through the audience that indicated the natives were restless.
Then I caught a wave of perfume. I stood up.

"How sweet of you, Mr. March," she said from behind me.
"How did you know it was me?"

I turned and looked at her. She had changed into an evening

---

* The actress Barrie Chase, one of the great dancers of movies and television,
retired from show business in 1972, whereas Julie Andrews remained active as a
performer into her later years.

gown that hid about as much of her as the G-string and pasties had. "I could hear the chants of Priapus,"* I told her.

That was a little over her head, but she knew it was a compliment and her eyes only blinked twice. "That's sweet of you," she said.

I thought it was myself, but I didn't say anything as I held the chair for her. She made quite a production out of sitting down. It gave me a fine view of the cleavage and the rest of the room an equally fine view of the other end. There was another audible sigh as I sat down next to her. I knew at that moment every man in the room hated me. It was a pretty good feeling.

The waiter appeared by magic. "Bring us a couple of drinks," I told him.

"What would you like, Miss LaSalle?"

"I'll have a French seventy-five," she said.

It was my turn to blink. She didn't look that stupid, so she had to be able to hold her drinks. It was made of champagne and brandy and had been about the most powerful thing around until the atom bomb was discovered. I swallowed once and said, "Make it two."

She looked at me with her big green eyes, her red hair swirling at she turned her head. "Oh, you like them, too? We must be soulmates. I'm just crazy about them."

"I knew you must be the minute I saw you," I said. I had just about decided that this interview wouldn't be too fruitful—but it would probably be fun.

The waiter came back with the drinks while she was still

---

* Ancient Greek god of fertility, depicted with a huge erection.

checking the room to make sure that she was getting enough attention.

Having a low and suspicious mind, I made one more maneuver. I lifted my glass. "Let's drink an old Silesian toast. On the first drink, we cross arms and you drink from my glass and I drink from yours. May our glasses never empty and our lips never dry."

"That's sweet," she said. I had a feeling I would hear that word several times during our conversation. She lifted her glass to my mouth and I lifted mine to her lips. We drank. I felt like a heel; her drink was the real thing. But I didn't let it bother me.

"How did you like the show?" she asked.

"The star attraction was great," I said. "The rest of it was five broads getting undressed."

She was pleased by that. "They're sweet kids," she said.

"Sure," I agreed.

"You said you wanted to talk to me, honey. Something about insurance?"

"That's right. I work for Intercontinental Insurance. We insured the Belters Building, which was burned down during the recent riots. We also insured the lives of two of the three men who died in the fire, Mr. Beld and Mr. Masters."

"You know, I thought you'd be a much older man. Not so young and handsome. I felt terrible about that accident. Mr. Masters was very sweet." There was no break between the two thoughts.

"I'm sure," I said. "Miss LaSalle, you own fifty-one percent of the stock. Right?"

"Yes, honey."

"It may be an indelicate question, but how did you get fifty-one percent?"

"He gave it to me, honey."

"That was … sweet of him," I said, wincing only slightly. "How active were you in the business?"

"Active? I didn't do anything. He made me sign a paper so he would run everything. He said it had to be done for income-tax reasons."

"Were you ever paid any money by the corporation?"

"No. But Mr. Masters was very generous."

"I'll bet he was. He went to Reno a short time before the recent accident. Did you go with him?"

"Of course, honey."

"Did Mr. Masters gamble while he was there?"

"Of course. That's why we went."

"Did he win or lose?"

"He won. He always won."

"How did you make out?"

"I won two jackpots," she said proudly.

"Great," I said. "On what? The nickel slots?"

"No. One on the half-dollar machine and one on a dollar machine. He gave me the money to play and I kept what I won."

I revised my estimate and came up with a new figure. She'd won about two thousand dollars. I should only be as stupid.

"Let's get back to the corporation," I said. I was beginning to feel I no longer controlled the conversation. "So you now own fifty-one percent of the company. And the paper you signed is no longer valid, since he's dead. Are you going to try to run the company?"

"Oh, no, honey. I don't know anything about business. I was thinking I'd sell my stock. Maybe to the widow. I figure it ought to be worth about ten million dollars. A girl ought to be able to get by on that."

"What'll you do then? Retire?"

"No, honey. My agent says he can get me a job in Paris right away."

"Why?" I asked. "With ten million dollars you don't have to work. You could retire and become the playgirl of the Western world."

"I guess so," she said doubtfully. "But I thought that would be for my old age. You know, like Social Security. Anyway, I like show business. I don't want to give that up until I get too old to perform. I figure this way I can work and not worry about getting stranded in some strange county. I'll always have the other money back here so there are no problems."

"I suppose you have a point," I said weakly.

The waiter must have been watching, because the minute she drained her glass he was there. "Two more, sir?" he asked, looking at me.

"Two more," I said. I finished mine before he was back with the fresh drinks, and waited until he'd left. "Miss LaSalle ... ," I began.

"Call me Sherry," she said.

"Okay, Sherry. How long did you know Mr. Masters?"

"About two years."

"When did he turn the stock over to you?"

"A little more than a year ago, I guess."

"Why did he do it?"

"I told you, honey. He said it had something to do with taxes. I don't know anything about business, so I didn't ask any questions."

"Did it ever occur to you that he was planning something at least unethical if not illegal, and if anything went wrong, you'd be blamed for it?"

The green eyes opened wide. "Oh, Harry would never do anything like that. He was too sweet."

"I know," I said wearily. "Did he ever talk to you about business?"

"I guess he did, honey, but I didn't listen much. All I know is he said everything was going great."

"Did he mean financially?"

"Of course. He was only interested in two things—business and me. He knew how things were going with me, so he must have been talking about the business."

"How were things going with you?"

"Fine, honey, just fine."

"Did he ever talk about quitting and going off to retire somewhere?"

"Oh, sure, he talked about it a lot. He was always going to take me with him. He said we'd go to South America or Europe and just have fun. But I told him I didn't want to give up my career. I think he was just talking anyway."

"Were you fond of him, Sherry?"

"Of course. He was—"

"I know," I interrupted hurriedly. "He hasn't been dead

very long, but I haven't seen any signs of mourning. Aren't you at least upset about his death?"

"Of course I am," she said indignantly. "I cried the whole morning when I heard about it. But a girl can't cry forever. Harry wouldn't have wanted me to, either. He'd want me to go on with my career. He thought I was a great artist."

"You're very brave," I said dryly.

"Thank you, honey." She finished her drink and glanced at her watch. "I have to get ready for the next show. I'll talk to you again later."

"I can't stay tonight," I told her. I decided I'd just about had it for one night. "I'll come back tomorrow."

"You promise?"

I nodded and stood up. I remained standing, and watched her walk away. They should have added a cover charge for that alone. When she was no longer in sight, I sat down and finished my drink, paid the check, and left just as the music was heralding the next show.

I drove straight back to the hotel and went into the bar for a couple of nightcaps. Then I stopped at the desk. There was a message for me. A George Henderson had called. That's all, no other message. It was too late for me to go back into the section of town where I'd probably find him, so I'd have to see him in the morning. I bought a paper and went up to my room.

There wasn't anything I could really pin together, but I had a feeling that I was getting close to the answers. It always worked like that on my cases. Just as you develop a feeling for cases that are sour, you also sense when you're working on the right track. That's when I get tense and nervous.

After skimming through the paper, I turned on the TV. I was only partly paying attention to the programs; the rest of me was concentrating on a building that had burned down and three men who had died in the fire. By this time I was certain it was no accident. That left me with a choice of two answers. Both were equally plausible.

One was that Harry Masters had deliberately faked his own death and put someone else in the building in his place. If that was true, it would be hard to prove, because the bodies were practically destroyed, so there was nothing to go on except their general size. There was another problem about that theory. Why? Offhand, I couldn't see any way he could get his hands on the insurance money. Even if Sherry LaSalle took or sent him her 51 percent of the stock, it seemed there was little he could do with it without betraying himself. If she managed to sell it for ten million dollars, it seemed less than he would have had if he'd stayed with a company he owned and ran.

The second possibility was that someone arranged for him to be killed. On that score there were only two likely suspects. One was his wife and the other was Sherry LaSalle, both of whom would gain. Or he could have been killed by someone who hated him. That made Kitty Harris a possibility, but there also might be a dozen other people scattered through town who had reason to hate him.

Either way, it meant I had a hell of a lot of work to do. I was still thinking about that when I fell asleep with the lights and the TV on.

The Today Show was on television when I awakened in the

morning. I glanced at my watch. It was only a few minutes after seven, but I knew I wouldn't be able to go back to sleep. I phoned room service and ordered breakfast and a bucket of ice. Then I took a fast shower, put on my shorts, and was watching the news when a knock sounded on the door. I let the waiter in and signed the check.

The news was over, so I turned the set off, poured a drink on the rocks for myself, and had a couple of swallows before I felt up to do anything else. Then I picked up the phone and put in a call to Martin Raymond in New York. He came on the line at once.

"Milo, boy," he said. "I called you yesterday."

"I know, but the factory was closed."

"How's it going?"

"Creeping along at a mad pace," I said. "You were right about one thing. It smells. So far all I have is a number of pieces that don't fit together. But I have a feeling I just might be able to save you all that loot."

"Great," he said. "I knew we could depend on you, Milo. Well, that's all I wanted to know. We're having a board meeting today, and I'll report we're making progress."

"You do that," I said. "And while we're on the subject of loot, you'd better send me some more money. I have to go up to Nevada today, and it's necessary to spread a little around down here, too."

He was so thrilled at the prospect of saving almost three million dollars he didn't even hesitate—much. "All right," he said. "I'll have my secretary wire you a thousand dollars today. Keep in touch, boy."

"Sure," I said. "Give my regards to the board. Tell them that luck and pluck always win out—at least according to Horatio Alger."* I hung up and turned my attention to breakfast.

I got dressed and went downstairs. An attendant brought my car around for me. I didn't see any sign of my shadows from the night before, but I suspected they'd show up before the day was over. When I'd worked on another case in Los Angeles a while back, I had talked to a detective in Hollywood several times. That was where I was going.

I didn't have to wait too long before I was told that Lieutenant Whitmore would see me. I went back and opened the door to his office. He was sitting at his desk, obviously making out a report. He looked up.

"Milo March," he said. "I know that name from somewhere. And the face that goes with it. ... I know. It was a couple of years ago. You're a private dick from New York or someplace, and you're working on a case here."

I nodded. "I am a private detective, but I only work on insurance cases. It was the Beverly Hills jewel job in which Johnny Renaldi was killed."**

"Yeah, that's the one. What are you doing out here now, March?"

"Working. I've run into a couple of men I'm interested in, and I thought you might know something about them."

"Who are they?"

---

* *Luck and Pluck* was one of a series of popular nineteenth-century children's books by Horatio Alger in which a poor boy succeeds thanks to determination and clean living. Milo himself embodies self-reliance and audacity; the absence of clean living doesn't seem to diminish his luck.
** See *The Day It Rained Diamonds* by M.E. Chaber.

"Gino Benetto and Joe Cabacchi, also known as Joe Cabbage."

He smiled. "You certainly pick some dandies to get interested in. They have records longer than both your arms. They've been arrested for almost everything in the book—speeding, resisting arrest, conspiracy to commit robbery, possession of stolen goods, blackmail, dealing in narcotics, living off the earnings of prostitutes, armed robbery, assault with a deadly weapon, manslaughter, and homicide. That's all I can think of at the moment."

"That's enough for now," I said. "Any convictions?"

"Not enough," he said grimly. "Benetto did one stretch for assault. Cabacchi served time for possession of narcotics and for carrying a gun. They beat all the other raps."

"Sounds like they have connections."

"The best that money can buy. We believe that they're partly in business for themselves and partly with the Syndicate—but we've never been able to prove very much. They're real tough babies. If you're brushing up against them, be sure to always keep your back to a wall. I notice you're carrying some extra weight. I seem to remember you had a license."

"That's right," I said. "Are they for hire?"

"For anything except honest work. They draw the line at that. What's the case you're working on?"

"Arson and murder—down in the southeast during the riots."

He whistled softly. "When you take a bite, you really get a mouthful, don't you? I've been working down there some since the riots. Almost every cop has. You know, there were dozens and dozens of fires set, and just as many acts of violence and looting. It was a mob of men, women, and children completely out of control. How do you expect to find which person or persons set one building on fire?"

"It all depends on whether my theory is right or not. I think the fire I'm interested in wasn't part of the riot, but was a separate act that took advantage of the riot to cover a more serious crime."

He thought about it for a minute. Then he nodded. "I can see it's possible—and clever. What about proof?"

"I don't have it yet, but I expect to get it. When I do, I'll put it in your lap. But I don't want to talk about it until it's more concrete."

"Okay," he said. "Where are you staying?"

"The Continental Hotel."

He made a note on a piece of paper. "How do Benetto and Cabacchi fit into this?"

"I don't know," I said honestly. "All I know is that they're very curious as to why I'm in that section of town. They've been following me practically since I've been here. That's enough to make me want to look into it a little more."

"Okay," he said. "Keep me informed. And good luck."

"Thanks," I said. "I'll see you around." Then I left. It was still early when I reached the southeast part of Los Angeles. I hoped that George would be around that early. I wasn't paying much attention to anything except where I was going, until I was about a block away from the bar. Then I realized there was a car keeping pace behind me. I recognized the car, too. It was the one that had followed me before. When

I swung into the curb and parked right in front of the bar, it pulled in behind me.

I got out of the car and looked around. There were no police in sight. By the time I'd reached the sidewalk, Benetto and Cabacchi were almost up to me.

"Hey, Mac," Benetto said, "we want to talk to you."

I wasn't going to run, so I turned to face them. Benetto walked up to me. His right hand was in his pocket, but I knew he was carrying his gun under his left arm, so I didn't worry about it too much. The other man walked around until he was in back of me.

"We asked you a question the other day," Benetto said. "You had to be a smart guy and not answer. Then yesterday we was around seeing what you were doing. You had to get smart and throw us off your tail."

"Sorry about that, chief," I said. "I don't know either one of you, and I don't see any reason why I should. Why don't you get lost?"

He laughed, but there was no humor in it. "We don't like a guy showing up wherever we are. I see you're wearing a piece, too. What are you—some kind of cop?"

"No kind of cop," I said. "You and your friend are carrying pieces. Are you some kind of cops?"

"What are you doing down here?"

"Minding my own business—like I told you the other day. You work your side of the street and I'll work mine."

"We work both sides of the street," he said flatly. "Don't forget that Joe has a piece on you—and he's a good shot. I'm going to teach you to mind your own business somewhere else. If there's a next time, we'll put you out of business." He took his hand out of his pocket and I saw his fingers were wrapped around a piece of pipe, with jagged ends sticking out of both sides of his hand.

"Just hold still, smart guy," he said. "This won't hurt— much." He took a sudden swing at me. I was watching, but I had thought he'd want to brag a little longer, so he caught me off guard.

I threw up one arm. It wasn't quite enough. His swing got over my arm and he hit me high on the cheekbone. It was hard enough to rock me and throw me back a step or two. As I straightened up, I could feel something warm trickling down my cheek.

He was starting to swing again, but this time I was ready for him. I blocked it with my left arm, then caught him with a fast right that twisted him around. I stepped in and hit him with a left that straightened him up, then swung my right as hard as I could into his stomach. I could hear the breath rushing out of his lungs as he started to bend in the middle. I grabbed his hair and yanked his head forward and down. At the same time, I brought my knee up to meet his face. Something like a sob came from his mouth as I shoved him away from me.

I didn't wait to admire the results. I took a quick step to the side and whirled around, reaching for my gun. I didn't see his friend at first. He was flat on the sidewalk, grunting with pain. Then I realized why. George Henderson and four of his friends had formed a ring around him, all of them grinning. George was rubbing the knuckles of his right hand.

"Welcome to the party, boys," I said.

"Thanks," George said, "but that other cat's got a gun he's trying to get out. I don't think our little old penknives are going to reach that far."

FIVE

That stopped me from celebrating. I turned back the other way, reaching for my holster. Benetto was on the sidewalk, blood streaming from his mouth and nose, but he was still trying to get that gun out. I pulled my own gun so that it was free of the holster. I knew he could see it, but I hoped that it was concealed enough so that it wouldn't be seen by anyone in a passing police cruiser.

"Want to try for the big prize, Gino?" I asked.

He glared at me, but his hand stopped moving. I stepped back so I could see both of the thugs—and so they could see I was armed. I took a quick look along the street. There were no cops in sight.

"Both of you," I said, "hit the road and fast. You stink up the neighborhood and I don't want to see you around. Besides, the cops are liable to get here soon. I have a permit for my gun; I'll bet you don't for yours."

They got to their feet, groaning, and edged toward the car. Benetto tried to say something, but the words got lost in the blood still coming from his mouth. His friend Joe took up the message.

"It's a good thing you had help," he said. "What are you? A nigger-lover?"

"No," I said. "I'm a people-lover. We're all pink on the

inside. But not you two. You're rotten-black inside and yellow stripes on the outside. Get going before I forget myself and start shooting. I don't want to awaken any late sleepers."

"We'll get you," Cabacchi said. "We're in no hurry, chum, but we'll get you."

"Okay," I said. "The next time it's for keeps. Be sure you both go to confession every day. I'd hate to think I killed you when you weren't ready. Now get moving or I won't wait for next time."

They climbed into their car and took off. I watched until they were well on the way, then shoved my gun back down into the holster. "Let's go have a drink. I've only had one this morning and I can't fly on one wing." The six of us went into the bar and sat down in the center. The bartender came up. "What happened?" he asked.

"You should've seen it, man," George said. "The five of us gave one cat his lumps, but this white boy brought religion to the other one. Chop-chop-wham and the cat was on the sidewalk gushing blood like a Texas oil well. Man, that was pretty. The two honkies wanted to get rough with some iron, but he chased them off like they was two kids who tried to eat all the ice cream at a birthday party."

"Sounds like a soul brother," the bartender said, and they all laughed.

"I'll be any kind of a brother if you'll give us something to drink," I said. "And count yourself in."

He started getting the drinks without asking what anybody wanted.

"Hey, George," one of the other men said, "where'd you find this whitey? He fights like he had religion."

"He ain't no whitey," George said. "He's an ofay." Everybody laughed, including me. George looked over. "In that pig Latin, how do you say black?"

"I never thought about it, but I guess it would be ackblay."

They laughed again. "Don't make any difference," George said, "because we're all pink on the inside. I think this boy's been messing around with some of our women." They all roared then.

The bartender brought the drinks. I put down ten dollars and lifted my glass.

"Thanks, men," I said.

"Just part of our community service," George answered. "If we'd stayed in here, only one man would have been messed up. This way there was two." He stopped and looked at me. "It seems to me that you're bleeding a little. Hey, fellows, did you notice he's got red blood, too?" They laughed again. A lot of it was nervous laughter, for they all knew it had been a sticky situation for a few minutes.

I finished my drink and put down the glass. "Give us another drink. All around." I took out my handkerchief and rubbed my cheek. It came away red.

"Must have cut myself shaving this morning," I said. "You can't trust these new blades. Everything's been improved."

The second round of drinks arrived.

One of the men raised his glass. "To the ofay," he said.

I drank. "I have a small speech to make," I said as I put down my glass.

"Hear, hear," George said.

I bowed my head gravely. "Thank you, sir. A very good

friend of mine told me about a seminar or discussion that took place in a local university about race relations. The group was addressed by a respected black scholar. At one point, and this may not be an exact quote, he said, 'We were raised to believe that white was wonderful and we were outcasts trying to glimpse this wonder. Now we have learned that black is beautiful.' My friend went up afterwards and handed a note to the scholar. On the paper she had written: 'If black is beautiful, does that mean that white is no longer wonderful?' He smiled and assured her that he meant to say that white was wonderful and black was beautiful. I would like to change this fine statement slightly. I would prefer to say that white is beautiful and black is beautiful—and that red is beautiful, yellow is beautiful, and brown is beautiful. If we had any people with green skins, I'm sure they would be beautiful. I suggest that in the future we drink to that."

Nobody said anything, but they all raised their glasses and we drank. I ordered another round and looked at George. I wasn't sure if I should mention that he had phoned me. He must have guessed what was on my mind.

"I wanted to see you," he said, "because we did pick up some information about the two men who were outside. I don't think it helps much, although it may explain why they're upset about you being around here."

"What is it?"

"You know there was considerable looting during the riots. We don't know who did it, but we have learned that these two have been going around buying a lot of the loot—mostly

TV sets, radios, watches, things like that. They haven't paid much, but they've taken away several carloads of stuff."

"How soon did they show up after the riots?" I asked.

"As a matter of fact," he said, "they were first seen here the night of the worst rioting. I don't think they stayed long, but they were here. Maybe they heard something in advance and came down to make a few contacts to buy, and then split." The others were nodding as he reported this.

"Thanks," I said. "I don't think that rules them out for the roles that I had in mind for them—but we'll see. I'm going to have to go now. I'm going out of town for a day or two. I'll be back down here as soon as I return."

"Okay," George said. "We'll see you."

They all said good-bye, even the bartender.

I went out, got in the car, and drove back to Wilshire. Near a phone booth, I parked and called the airport to check on planes to Reno. I made a reservation for one in early afternoon. I thought that gave me enough time. Then I looked up the phone number of Harry Masters. I dialed it and a woman answered.

"Mrs. Masters?" I asked.

"Yes. Who is this?"

"Milo March. Remember I'm the man from the insurance company who was out to see you the other day? Yesterday, in fact."

"Oh, yes. I remember you, Mr. March. What can I do for you?"

"I wondered if you have a recent photo of your husband?"

"Yes," she said, "I believe there is one. He had a photograph taken for some brochure the corporation put out. He had the original framed and placed it in his room. Harry liked to admire himself."

"Could I borrow it for a few days? I promise to return it."

"Of course you may. You don't have to return it. I intend to have the maid come and clean up the room anyway."

"Is it convenient if I show up now?"

"Yes. I'll expect you, Mr. March." She hung up.

I went back to the car and drove west on Wilshire until I reached her address, parked, and entered the building. Mrs. Masters met me at the door. I went in and sat on the same couch.

"I have the photograph here, Mr. March," she said. "I thought you wouldn't want the frame, so I removed it." She picked up a photograph and held it out.

I took it. He looked much as I would have expected, a little heavy around the jowls, with the determined stare of the successful tycoon. No humor or joy. It was a ruthless face.

"I haven't been in his room for years," she said. "It certainly is a mess of things, all of them unimportant, I'm sure. I'll have the maid throw out everything."

"Would you do me a favor, Mrs. Masters?"

"What?"

"I'll be out of town for a day or two. Will you let me go through your husband's room when I get back, and delay letting the maid throw anything away until I've had a look?"

"Why?"

"I don't know what I want to look for, but I'm hoping that I'll find something that will help. I know that there are two criminals, both with long records, who visited your husband once at his office and who were also in the neighborhood the night of the fire. Both men have committed murder and probably will again, but they've never been convicted of a killing. I'd like to go through your husband's room just to see if he might have scribbled a note, or something that will give me a clue to what they were doing."

"Have you discussed the two men with the police?"

"Yes. But they have even less information than I do, and there are no grounds for arresting them at this time."

"All right, you may go through the room when you return."

"Thank you, Mrs. Masters. I'll call you as soon as I get back."

"Very well."

I went downstairs and drove to the hotel, stopping in a luggage shop to buy an attaché case. Up in my room, I packed the few things I'd need to take with me, adding the photograph of Masters. Then I phoned Sherry LaSalle. She sounded half asleep when she answered.

"Milo March," I said. "Did I awaken you?"

"It's all right, honey. You can wake me up anytime."

"I'll keep that in mind," I said. "I called to tell you that I'm going out of town today and will be back tomorrow or, at the latest, the following day. And I'll be at the club that night."

"I was looking forward to seeing you tonight," she said in a little-girl voice. "But you will come when you get back?"

"Promise," I said. "Good-bye."

"Bye, honey."

It was lunchtime. I took the attaché case and went downstairs, stopping at the desk. The clerk handed me a Western Union envelope containing my expense money from Intercontinental. I told him that I wasn't checking out, but would be out of town for one or two days.

Stopping at the Western Union office, I cashed the money order after a short hassle over the amount. Then I drove on down to the Casa Del Monte. Bo was working. He nodded in my direction and brought me a martini.

"What happened to you?" he asked, looking at my cheekbone.

"Ran into a piece of pipe. A guy was holding it."

"Benetto?"

"The same."

"How does *he* look?"

"I'm not sure. The last time I saw him there was too much blood to tell. But I imagine he lost a few teeth, among other things."

"What have you got in the fancy luggage, a machine gun?"

"Just some clothes. I'm going to Reno for a day or two."

"To gamble?"

"No. Work. The man I'm interested in went there fairly often. I don't know where he gambled, but he did some of his drinking at a place called The Sewer."

"I know it well. On Second Street. If you want to see the owner, he works the morning shift—eight to four. He's known as Crooked Ted, sometimes as Teddie. If you see him, tell him I said hello. You'd better say Leonard because they don't know me up there as Bo. Teddie's a good guy. If he can help you, he will."

"I'll remember. Thanks."

I had two more martinis and then some lunch. I told Bo I'd see him when I got back and left, stopping at the local five-and-ten to pick up a large manila envelope. In my car I opened the attaché case and put the manila envelope inside. Then I drove to the airport. I arranged to park my car until I returned, picked up my ticket, and went to the bar to wait for boarding time.

It was a short flight to Reno. The plane swooped over the mountains and then seemed to drop straight down. I was glad I didn't have a drink in my hand. I also made a mental note never to fly into Reno again—at least, not from Los Angeles.

I got a taxi at the airport and told the driver to take me to a good motel within walking distance of the casinos.

He nodded. "There's a good one at Fourth and Virginia," he said. "You'll be three blocks from some of the biggest casinos. Okay?"

"Fine," I said.

It was a short drive from the airport. The motel looked all right from the outside, so I paid off the driver and went in. The room was fine and I took it for one or two nights. When I was alone, the first thing I did was to remove my shoulder holster and put it and the gun in the attaché case. I probably wouldn't need it while I was here.

It was still early in the afternoon, so I took off my coat and stretched out on the bed. It was six o'clock when I awakened. I slipped into my jacket and went out to look at the city.

The casino signs were clearly visible from the motel. By the time I'd walked two blocks, the sounds were equally audible. I could hear the keno numbers being called over a loudspeaker and the hum of hundreds of slot machines. Then I could see the grim-faced players, mostly middle-aged women, standing rigidly in front of one or two machines. They played with the blank concentration of robots, and the wheels whirred in a deadly rhythm that seemed to fit the picture. As I walked along, I saw two women hit jackpots. Their faces showed no elation; they just scooped up the coins and started feeding them back into the same machines. Finally I reached Second Street and stopped to look around. I spotted The Sewer. It was just across the street.

When the light changed, I walked over. It was a good-sized place with lights so dim I could hardly see. When my eyes finally adjusted, I saw that it was just a bar—no gambling, no food, just booze. There were maybe fifteen people sitting at the bar, men and women. They didn't look like high-rollers and they were fairly young. I guessed they were probably people who worked in the casinos and were either finishing a shift or taking a coffee break. I picked a stool at the end of the bar as the bartender came over.

"Gin and grapefruit juice," I said.

He nodded and poured the drink. I gave him a dollar and he brought back forty cents in change. So the prices were right.

"Is Crooked Ted working tomorrow morning?" I asked.

"He is if he makes it. You a friend of his?"

"No, but we have a mutual friend who told me to look him up when I got here."

"He'll probably make it. He doesn't always finish the shift, but he usually starts it." He walked back down the bar to wait on another customer.

I sipped my drink and listened to the conversation. There was a high percentage of four-letter words from both the men and women, but they used them about the same way other people would say "damn." There was also a lot of talk about various clubs, so my guess about their professions was apparently right.

The bartender came back and put another drink in front of me.

"What's that?" I asked.

"One of the boys had a little luck on the dice tables and he bought the house a drink."

"Tell him I said thanks."

He nodded and moved away. After he collected for the drinks, he came back. I noticed he had a drink in his hand. "You're new around here, aren't you?" he asked.

"Yeah. Just got in a couple of hours ago."

"Try your luck yet?"

"No. I don't do much of that. Besides, I'll only be here one or two days. Gambling is like a woman; you need plenty of time."

"And you usually lose," he said. He drifted away again.

I finally finished my second drink and motioned for him. When he got back, I said, "Give the bar a drink and count yourself in."

He nodded and went to make the drinks. He must have told them who was buying, for several customers raised their glasses to me in thanks. Finally he made one for me and poured himself a shot of bourbon. He came over and put both drinks down.

"Good luck," he said. Then he took my money and rang up the sale. "Where you from?"

"I'm from New York, but I came here from Los Angeles."

"I used to work down there," he said, "but I like it up here."

"Looks like it's a sort of neighborhood bar," I said.

He nodded. "We get a lot of the people who work in the casinos. They come in here on their coffee breaks, when they get off shift, sometimes before they go on. We more or less take care of them. When they get drunk, we get a taxi to take them home. When they win at the tables and come in to get drunk, we take most of their money away from them and give it back the next day. When they go broke at the tables, they come in and run up a tab or borrow money."

"Sounds like one big happy family." I finished my drink and pushed a dollar across the bar. "Well, I'll see you."

"Thanks for coming in," he said.

I went across the street to Harrah's Club, found a seat at a 21 table, and played a few hands. My heart wasn't in it, so I lost about five dollars. Then I got up and found a table in the dining room. I had a martini and dinner. The food was good and the price was low, but then they made their money on gambling.

After dinner I went back to the 21 tables. This time I did a little better. I didn't play long, but I had won twenty dollars when I quit. I bought a San Francisco paper, some cigarettes, and a bottle of V.O. and went back to the motel. There was an ice machine and I bought a pitcher of ice cubes and then went to my room to get undressed. I made a drink, turned on the TV, and stretched out on the bed with the paper. I felt like a quiet evening at home. Besides, I wanted to be up early the next morning.

A couple of hours later I decided I was tired enough. I went into the bathroom and examined my face. The cut was nothing, but my cheek was turning a variety of colors. There wasn't much I could do about that, so I went back to the room and went to sleep.

It was six-thirty when I opened my eyes. That was just about right. I shaved and showered and got dressed. Then I took the photograph from my attaché case and slipped it in the manila envelope. I walked down the street and stopped in one of the casinos. All the slot machines were still going madly and there were people hunched over tables. In the dining room almost everyone was playing keno while they ate breakfast. I had the strange feeling that the madness never stopped. As a matter of fact, it probably didn't, since everything was open twenty-four hours a day.

After breakfast I walked down to The Sewer. It was a little after eight when I sat down at the bar. There were a dozen others there, looking as if it were the end of the day for them. The tall, good-looking man behind the bar was drinking coffee and talking to one of the customers. He finished whatever he was saying before he came up to me.

"Good morning, sir," he said.

"Good morning. I'll have a gin and grapefruit juice, in an old-fashioned glass, please."

I usually don't drink in the morning, but I'll force one down. I waited until he put my drink down. "Have one yourself."

He lifted a bottle of brandy and poured a shot into his

coffee. Then he took my money and rang up the sale.

"You're Crooked Ted, aren't you?" I asked as he brought my change.

He looked at me. "You're new in here, so someone must have been talking behind my back. I'm Crooked Ted."

"A friend of mine in Los Angeles told me to look you up. He's Leonard Del Monte. My name is Milo March."

We shook hands. "If Leonard is a friend of yours, then you must be about crazy enough to wind up in this joint without being sent. How is Leonard?"

"Fine. As a matter of fact, I intended to come here even if he hadn't mentioned you."

"Is the joint getting that famous? I'll have to sell it and get a quieter place."

"I heard about it because a man I'm interested in used to come here."

"A man you're interested in? Are you some kind of a cop?"

"I'm not a cop. I work for an insurance company. This man has carried several policies with us for some time." I took the photograph from the envelope and put it on the bar. "Do you recognize him?"

"Sure. I don't remember his last name at the moment, but his first name is Harry. He used to come up here about once a month—a heavy player and a heavy spender. I don't know why, but he started coming in here when he wasn't at the tables. What's this all about? I wouldn't want to get him in trouble. I kind of liked the guy."

"Well, if we can believe the official reports, he's beyond getting in trouble."

"What do you mean?"

"According to the police reports and everyone else, he's dead."

"No. What happened? He was up here only a couple or three weeks ago. He seemed all right then."

"Did you read about the riots in Los Angeles?"

He nodded.

"One of the buildings that was burned down was owned by him. It was completely destroyed. When they went through the ashes, they found the remains of three bodies. There wasn't enough left to make any positive identification, but it is believed the bodies were those of this man, his brother-in-law, and the night watchman. Incidentally, his last name was Masters." I put the photograph back in the envelope.

"Yeah, that's it. What are you doing, contesting the claims?"

"We don't know yet. A couple of things bother us. Even though there are witnesses who say they spoke to him by phone shortly before the fire and he was then in the building, there's no real proof that he died there. Then, too, we know of a couple of hoods who at least knew Masters and who were seen in the vicinity of the building shortly before it was burned. So he might have been killed and the building set on fire to cover a murder. He did have a lot of money and property. And the two hoods don't like anyone snooping around. That's how I got this cheekbone."

"Nice colors," he said. "It goes well with your shirt." He poured me a fresh drink and put some more brandy in his coffee. "Who collects the bread?"

"Part of the insurance money goes to his wife and part to his corporation. But the interesting thing is that he didn't own a controlling interest in the corporation."

"Who did?"

"A broad named Sherry LaSalle. A redheaded stripper who was his favorite shack job at the moment. I think he brought her up here a few times."

He nodded. "I remember there was a redheaded broad with him sometimes. How'd she get him to do that? I thought he was pretty shrewd."

"Apparently he was—most of the time. He turned fifty-one percent of the stock over to the broad more than a year ago, but he made her sign a proxy giving him the right to vote the stock, so it was safe enough as long as he was alive. Now the proxy is no good, if he's dead and she's still got the stock. I'm told that the corporation is worth thirty or forty million dollars."

"That's a lot of bread. And, as I remember her, she was a lot of broad. Half of thirty million is fifteen million. People have been killed for less. So he had a wife, too?"

"Yeah. Not much happened between them for years. She says he was a lousy lay and doesn't seem to care. She's a shrewd cookie herself and made some smart investments out of money he gave her over the years. But I'm sure she'd rather have the rest of the money than have it go to another woman."

"Who wouldn't? What are you looking for here?"

"I don't know. I'm just trying to get as complete a picture as I can and hope something falls into place."

"Hey, Teddie," a customer called. "How about a little service down here?"

"You're already getting about as little as I can give you," he said. He walked down to the customer. "Are you buying the house a drink? After all, my friend up there came all the way from Los Angeles, and I wouldn't want him to think that we're unfriendly."

"If that's the only way I can get a drink, okay. Give every-body a drink. But when is the house going to buy?"

"I wouldn't know. I was just sent out here this morning by the union hall."

He made drinks for everybody, including some more brandy in his coffee, and collected for them. Then he came back to me.

"I don't think I know anything that will help," he said. "Like I told you, he seemed a nice guy—a plunger and a spender. He'd come in here, buy six or seven rounds for the bar, and talk. Then he'd leave ten or twenty as a tip and go back to the tables for a couple of hours."

"What did he talk about?"

"Mostly gambling and broads. I got the idea that he liked broads—in the plural."

"How'd he do gambling? Was he a winner or a loser?"

"Mostly a winner. The last time he was here, he said he won thirty thousand. A pit boss from across the street told me that was about right. Which reminds me of something. He was here about two months ago. The broad wasn't with him. He was nervous and restless. The second day he was here, he hit the tables for fifty thousand. What do you think he did?"

"What?"

"He took me, one of my bartenders, and a friend of mine

from California, and the four of us took a plane to Paris, with him picking up the tab for everything. It's a good thing we had passports or we would have blown the whole trip."

"How long were you gone?"

"Only a few days. We stayed in Paris long enough to clear through the officials and then we went to Monte Carlo. That's where he wanted to go and that's where we stayed until he decided to come back. But he wouldn't let anyone pay for anything. We all had a great time. He was like a kid. I remember that when we were coming back he said if he ever decided to retire, Monte Carlo was where he wanted to live."

"How did he make out on the gambling there?"

"He won. I saw him win a bundle, and he said he made money on the trip. He claimed he was lucky whenever it came to money. I guess he was right."

"Maybe," I said.

"I'll tell you something else about him. We have a fellow up here named Freddie Freeman. We call him Freddie the Freeloader. He used to be a racehorse trainer, but he'd been a bum for fifteen years. A big fellow. I'm always chasing him out because he tries to mooch drinks from the customers. Harry always slipped him twenty or fifty bucks every time he saw him. Haven't seen him since the last time Harry was here."

"What happened?"

"I don't know. Freddie had some family back in Cleveland, Ohio. He hadn't seen them in years and was always talking about going. I think Harry put him on a plane with some pocket money, and sent him home. I know he said he was going to."

"The last time Harry was here, did he say anything about when he'd be back?"

"Yeah. He said he'd see me in three or four weeks."

"I guess he won't make it now," I said. "Anything else about him?"

"I don't think so," he answered. "He seemed to have only three interests in life—money, gambling, and broads. He did say a couple of times he was thinking of moving his offices up here. But I guess he forgot about it."

"I can't put him down because of his interests. Better give all of us another drink—including yourself."

"I always pour my own first." He served the drinks and took my money.

"Ever hear of two hoods named Benetto and Cabacchi? The second one is sometimes known as Joe Cabbage."

"I don't think so," he said. "Local boys?"

"Mostly Los Angeles. I just thought I'd ask. Was Harry friendly with anyone else?"

"He might have been. He was a friendly guy. But I don't know of anyone. He spent all his time at the tables, in here, or with a broad. I know he went to a house up in Sparks occasionally when he didn't have a broad with him. But I don't know who he saw up there."

"Okay," I said. I finished my drink. "Thanks, Teddie. I'll see you."

"Right. Come around anytime. We always have a floor show—put on by the customers. If I don't see you before you go back, say hello to Leonard for me."

"Will do," I said. I left my change on the bar and walked out.

I visited most of the big casinos after that. I'd play a few games of 21, shoot some craps, and show the photograph to the dealers and the pit bosses. A number of them recognized Masters, but they couldn't tell me anything except that he was a plunger, that he usually won and was generous with tips when he did. It didn't add much. Finally I gave up. I thought I might have something, but I wasn't sure what it was.

I phoned the airport. I could get a plane back to Los Angeles in a little more than two hours. I had some lunch and then went back to the motel and packed—not forgetting to put the bottle of V.O. in the attaché case. I checked out and called a cab.

Just before we took off, I suddenly remembered the drop when we came in to land. I got the bottle out and took a strong drink. Then I went to sleep before we had to make that big leap.

It was early in the evening when we landed. I got my car and drove straight to the hotel. There was a message for me. I didn't look at it until I got up to my room. Then I opened it. Someone had called to tell me that George Henderson had been shot and was in the County Hospital. That was all.

SIX

The time schedule was blown up. I took a minute to strap on the shoulder holster, check my gun, and slip it into the holster. I stopped down at the desk long enough to get the directions to County. Then I took off and pushed the Cadillac as hard as I could until I reached the hospital. I parked and rushed in, demanding to see Henderson.

I was shown into a room with four beds, all of them occupied. I spotted George in the bed on the left. Someone was with him, but when I showed up, George said something and the man stood up. He passed me as I headed for George. He didn't look too friendly. I stopped beside the bed.

"How are you?" I asked abruptly.

He grinned at me. "Fine," he said. "I was shot through the left shoulder. No bones broken, just a clean wound. The only thing is that the cops think that I must have started something and that's why I was shot. After all, a black man down in that section must have a chip on his shoulder, and if there's any trouble, he must have started it."

"I'll take care of that," I said. "Who was it? The Silver Dust Twins* from yesterday morning?"

"I think so. The car looked like the one they were driving.

---

* This is a play on the "Gold Dust Twins," caricatures of two black children who appeared as brand mascots for cleaning products from 1903 till the mid-1950s. Milo substitutes the word "Silver" to refer to the two white gangsters.

I was walking along the street and this car came up behind me. That's where they shot me from—the back. Then the car took off."

"How are you really? Need any blood or anything?"

"Nothing, man. Except maybe some cigarettes later."

"Do they come around with cigarettes?"

"Yeah. Somebody said they'll be here in another hour. That's plenty of time."

I pulled out some money and put two tens on the table next to his bed.

"Here," I said. "You may want to get a newspaper, too."

He laughed. "Man, that'll be some newspaper. I don't need that much money. I'll be out of here by tomorrow unless the fuzz takes a dim view."

I made a brief suggestion about the fuzz. "I'll take care of that, so you'll be out. Where can I find you when you leave?"

"In the bar, I guess."

"Okay, when you go, call my hotel and just give them your name. Then I'll know you're out. How much are they charging you for the hospital?"

"They shouldn't charge nothing. I'm not working, so it should be free."

"Frig 'em," I said. I pulled out my money and found a fifty-dollar bill. I put it next to the two tens. "Pay them and tell them to go screw. It's on the expense account."

"You don't have to—" he began.

"Screw you, too," I said. "Look, boy, don't talk back to a white man."

"Yes, suh, boss," he said with a grin.

"I'm going back to work. I'll see you sometime tomorrow. Want me to smuggle some booze in to you?"

"No, thanks. I'll wait until tomorrow. They got too many other shots in me."

"Okay. I'll see you tomorrow." I winked at him and left.

I drove back to the hotel and went up to my room. First I called Lieutenant Whitmore. He was still in his office.

"This is Milo March," I said. "Remember our conversation about Benetto and Cabacchi?"

"Yes."

"Yesterday morning they attacked me in southeast Los Angeles. I got one clip on the side of the face and it is now several colors of the rainbow. With the help of a Negro named George Carver Henderson, I chased them off. They drove away, swearing to get even. This morning, George Henderson was shot through the left shoulder by two men in a car like the one those two men are driving. He is in County Hospital. I am told that the police are insisting that he must have started a fight, because he was shot in the Negro community, and that they're trying to hold him. That's nonsense. He didn't start any fight and he's not going to run away. If you want to charge him with anything, do so and I'll go his bail. If not, let him go home from the hospital tomorrow as he's supposed to."

"Hold on," he said. "I don't know anything about the case, but I'll check on it. If what you say is true, I'll see that he's released. If it's not true, I'll notify you of the charge and the amount of the bail. Fair enough?"

"Okay. I'm at the Continental Hotel."

I hung up, waited a minute, and then called The Bodies

and made a reservation for just before the last show. I asked for the same table I had had before and requested that Miss LaSalle be told I had made the reservation.

Then I called room service and told them to send up a newspaper and a bucket of ice. I kicked off my shoes and waited, realizing that I was tired. It had been a long day and was about to be longer before it was through. I would have time for a nap if I waited for my dinner. The stripper would probably be hungry, and I could eat with her.

The waiter arrived with the paper and ice. I poured a drink on the rocks and read the paper. There wasn't much in it. I threw it to one side and let my mind wander over the case. I'd been spreading the murder theory around, but I didn't believe it myself. It only served one purpose. It made people more willing to talk. If they thought I was accusing someone they knew, a respectable businessman, of deliberately burning down a building and killing three people in order to defraud an insurance company, the shock of the charge would make them clam up. If they thought he'd been murdered, they'd be eager to help.

Instinct and logic told me that the idea that Harry Masters had been murdered was out. Who would have done it and why? His wife would gain some money through his death, but not enough to risk murder. She would have just as much with him alive as dead, maybe more. And Sherry LaSalle? She still had the stock. Alive, he did hold a proxy on the voting rights, but he couldn't exercise that if he was pretending to be dead. He couldn't force her to return the stock. He couldn't stop her from selling it. If she sold it, he couldn't even make her give him the money or any part of it.

What, I thought, if the stock was worthless? If no one else knew it, she could still sell the stock for a good price, but the stakes had to be higher than that. And higher than the personal account and the special account which had been cleaned out. I decided I'd have to give some attention to the financial picture. I poured a second drink and leaned back again.

The telephone rang. I picked it up.

"March, this is Lieutenant Whitmore," he said. "I've been checking on that shooting you told me about. First, I also got a report on that fracas with Benetto and Cabacchi yesterday. There was a witness who phoned the police and said that three white men and five Negroes had a fight on the street. When the cops showed up, there was no one there, but they did find a considerable amount of blood on the sidewalk in front of a local bar. They went in and questioned the men who were there. They all denied knowing anything about any fight. One of the men was this George Henderson."

"I don't see where that has anything to do with his being shot."

"Wait a minute. George Henderson is someone we strongly suspect had an active part in the riot. He wasn't arrested and we can't prove it. We can believe that he was involved in a fight with white men and that was why he was shot. He won't name who shot him, so we can only think that he wants to continue the fight himself."

"That's no reason to curtail his movements without making a charge against him."

"Okay," he said with a sigh. "He'll be permitted to leave the hospital whenever the doctors say it's okay. But the officers down in that area will keep watch on him. You know, you could do a lot to help the situation."

"Me? How?"

"By coming in and signing a complaint against Benetto and Cabacchi for their attack on you."

"Nonsense," I said. "You and I both know that they would beat that rap. And it would bring me out in the open. Then they'd know why I'm here. As it is, they're only guessing. And I want to get enough on them so I can hand them over to you on a much more serious charge than simple assault."

"All right. But don't come running to us with any story about being picked on unless you're willing to sign a complaint. We're paid to work, not to pull your chestnuts out of the fire."

"Right, Lieutenant. And thanks. I'll be in touch."

"Do that," he said dryly, and hung up.

I finished my drink and went to sleep.

When I woke up two hours later, I was feeling much better. I went into the bathroom and checked my face. I didn't need a shave and my cheekbone was looking a little better, so I undressed, took a shower, and dressed again. I made a pile of dirty clothes and phoned the valet service, asking them to pick up the laundry and my suit and have them back for me the next day. It was still too early to go to The Bodies, so I drove down to Del Monte's in Hollywood.

Bo wasn't working, but he was on the other side of the bar. I took the stool next to him and ordered drinks for the two of us.

"How was Crooked Ted?" he asked.

"He sent his regards to you," I said. "That's quite a joint he runs."

"Did you learn anything?"

"I think so, but I'm not quite sure what. Sometimes it goes on like that for days and then lightning strikes. Or it gets worse. Have you seen our friend?"

"He hasn't been in, but I saw him going down the street. His face didn't look too good."

"It looks better than it should."

"I told you he was a tough boy and he's got connections. You may be getting into something you don't know about."

I laughed. "If there's anything in his line that I don't know, it hasn't been invented. And I've got more Syndicate notches on my gun than any other kind. He and his friend and I have all agreed that the next time we tangle, it'll be for keeps."

"Remind me," he said, "not to accept any rides from you for a while."

I had two more drinks, sipping them slowly, then decided it was late enough for me to go to The Bodies. I said good night and left.

I was escorted to the same ringside table I'd had before. While I was waiting, I ordered a bourbon on the rocks. It wasn't long before the show started. The same five girls came out and went through the weary business of taking their clothes off. They made faces and wriggled their bodies, but it was all about as exciting as watching your grandmother get ready for bed.

Then there was the big buildup, the fanfare, and Sherry

came on. I had to admit that she had more than a beautiful figure. And she was more than graceful at removing her clothes. There was some kind of fire that reached out and enveloped the audience. I suspected she would have projected the same thing if she did a different act.

She finished to loud applause and disappeared behind the curtains. It wasn't long before she came through the back door and over to my table. She was wearing a simple but attractive green dress and a few pieces of jewelry; there was an almost scrubbed look to her face. She was lovely to look at. I stood up and held the chair for her, enjoying the sighs of envy around the room.

"Hello, Milo," she said. "I was hoping you'd be here." The waiter showed up. I looked at her. "A French seventy-five," she said.

"Two of them?" the waiter asked.

"Not on an empty stomach," I said. "I'll have another bourbon on the rocks." I waited until he'd left. "Have you had dinner, Sherry?"

"No, honey. I never eat until after the last show. But let's not eat here. I know a nice little place not far away. We'll go there after we finish our drinks. How was your trip, honey?"

"Fine."

"Where did you go?"

"Reno." I had decided to tell her part of the truth. If she was involved in anything, it might shake her up a little.

"A fun trip?" she asked casually.

"Partly. I played a few times at the tables, talked to a few people, and caught the next plane back."

"Did you win?"

"A little."

"I just love Reno," she said dreamily. "Harry used to take me there."

"I know."

She looked at me suddenly and there was shrewdness in her eyes. "Is that why you went up there, honey? To ask about Harry?"

"That's why. I wanted to see if he'd had any enemies there."

"Harry didn't have any enemies anywhere."

"Well, it certainly wasn't friends who burned down that building with three men in it. Besides, no man makes several million dollars without also making a few enemies."

"You think someone meant to kill Harry?"

"It's very possible," I said. "Did you ever know him to have anything to do with two men named Gino Benetto and Joe Cabacchi?"

"No," she said firmly. "I'm sure he never knew anyone with names like that. Who are they?"

"Hoods."

"No. Harry never knew any gangsters. He didn't even like for me to work in nightclubs because he said a lot of gangsters went to them. I told him they never bothered me, so he finally dropped it."

"Then we'll switch the question," I said with a smile. "Did you ever meet the two men I mentioned?"

"No, honey. If they went to clubs, maybe I saw them some time or other, but I don't know those names. Why?"

"I just wondered," I said. "Let's finish our drinks and go

have some dinner."

I beckoned the waiter and paid the bill. Then we went out to my car. I held the door for her, then went around and slipped in. "Tell me where to go."

"Turn to the right when you leave the parking lot. It's only a few blocks from here. You know, honey, I called the club before I came to work tonight. They told me that you had made a reservation, so I took a cab instead of driving my car. I thought you might drive me home."

She probably knew damn well I'd drive her home, but I only nodded. She directed me to the right and we went about five blocks before she told me to stop. It was a small but fashionable-looking building. I parked and we went inside. It was an intimate little place. Despite the late hour there were several diners there.

She ordered another French seventy-five and I switched to a dry martini. After the first drink we ordered two more and our dinner. She'd been right about one thing. The food was delicious. She chattered, mostly about show business, as we ate. It was after one-thirty when we finally left. She told me where she lived. It was a new, modern apartment house.

"Why don't you come up for a nightcap?"

"All right," I said. I parked behind a bright red Rolls.

"That's my car, honey," she said. "Isn't it sweet?"

I admitted it was sweet and we went upstairs. Her apartment was large and furnished in good taste, but there were enough things tossed around in it to give a rumpled look.

"Come in the kitchen," she said, "and we'll make two French seventy-fives."

This time I didn't protest, but followed her into the kitchen. I wasn't that crazy about them, but I was damned if I would let a broad drink me under the table. She opened the door of the refrigerator. It was almost full of champagne. The only food in it was some yogurt, milk, and two tomatoes.

She told me where the brandy was in the closet, which was as full of brandy as the refrigerator was of champagne. The girl didn't believe in running short on the essentials. I watched while she made the drinks, then we carried them into the living room.

"You like my little apartment?" she asked.

"Yes." Then I decided to beat her to the punch. "It's sweet."

"Thank you, honey," she said. She was obviously pleased I had learned to talk her language. "Do you mind if I go slip into something more comfortable?"

"Go ahead."

She got up and walked into what was apparently the bedroom. I turned my attention to the room I was in. There wasn't too much to see except furniture and some stock pictures on the walls. There were ashtrays, a box of cigarettes, and a lighter on the coffee table. Across the room there was a small desk. A framed photograph of Harry Masters was on it, a telephone, and a pile of papers. I would have liked to look through the papers, but thought I wouldn't have enough time before she came back.

I was right. She came into the room just as I was having the thought. She had changed into something that may have made her more comfortable, but it certainly didn't do the same for me. It looked more like a nightgown—and a thin one at that—than anything else. I didn't need perfect vision to see that the only thing under it was Sherry.

"This is better," she said. She lifted her glass. "Let's drink to us."

We did. "You're sweet," she continued. "Sometime you must tell me all about your work. It must be fascinating—sort of like being a detective."

I grunted an answer, but she wasn't even listening. She continued to chatter through three more French seventy-fives—each. I was beginning to wish that I had insisted on having straight brandy. She was putting them down like water, and the only change I could see was that her eyes were brighter. Then, suddenly, she put the glass down and stood up.

"Let's make love," she said simply. She turned and walked into the bedroom.

It's difficult to be rude to a lady in circumstances like that. I set my glass on the coffee table and followed her. By the time I'd reached the bedroom she had shed the nightgown. I didn't have long to contemplate her beauty. She came up, put her arms around my neck, and lifted her face. I kissed her.

The fire I'd noticed in her before wasn't confined to the stage. It reached out and pulled me into the flames. I was having a little trouble breathing by the time she drew back. She laughed deep in her throat and fell on the bed. I didn't look at her while I undressed. Then I was on the bed and she was in my arms.

The fire was still there. It was not so intense, but was building slowly. I responded to it. It wasn't long before somewhere in the back of my mind there was the realization that if I had 51 percent of any stock, I would also give it to her. Or even a 100 percent. …

Later, much later, I remembered her sighing, then curling up and going to sleep. I must have gone to sleep at once myself.

It was daylight when I awakened. I glanced at my watch—eight o'clock. She was still sleeping, in the same position. I quietly got out of bed and started to dress. Halfway, my attention was caught by brightly colored papers on the stand next to her bed. I went around to look at them. There were three maps—one was of the city of Paris, one of Rome, and one of Monaco. They were typical travel maps. And she had said her agent was getting her a job in Paris.

I finished dressing and was just shrugging into my jacket when she opened one green eye. "Where you going, honey?" she asked sleepily.

"I have to go to work. I'll call you later."

"All right. Good night." She went back to sleep just like that.

I went into the living room and stopped at the sight of the desk. I listened. She was breathing evenly with just a slight suggestion of a snore. I moved quietly over to the desk and began looking at her papers. They were mostly bills. There was one letter from a girl who was playing a club in Chicago. There was a telephone bill, postmarked only two days earlier. I looked at it. There were three long-distance calls on it—one to New York and then, three days later, two to Paris. They might mean nothing. I memorized the two numbers anyway. Then I let myself out and closed the door gently.

When I got downstairs, I wrote the two numbers in my address book. Then I drove back to my hotel and went straight up to my room. I showered and shaved and put on fresh clothes before pouring myself a drink without ice. I could still feel the echo from those French seventy-fives and I needed some medicine.

Then I went to the phone and put in a station-to-station call to the New York number. It was answered by an operator in a hotel. I hung up gently. I waited a few minutes, working on the drink, then put in a station-to-station call to the number in Paris. This was also a hotel, but this time I decided to talk to them.

"Do you have," I asked in my best French, "a Miss Sherry LaSalle registered there, or do you have a reservation for her?"

"Just a minute," the operator said. She came back on the phone in about two minutes. "Miss LaSalle is not here, but she does have a reservation for the twenty-second of this month."

"Thank you," I said. "I just wanted to be sure there was a confirmation of her arrival." I hung up. The twenty-second was about two and a half weeks off. I'd have to ask her about when her engagement in Paris started.

Next I phoned Mrs. Masters. She answered the ring promptly.

"This is Milo March," I said. "I wondered if I could come out sometime today to go through Mr. Masters's room."

"Well," she said, "I won't be home this afternoon, but you can come out this morning if that's convenient. It won't take long, will it?"

"It shouldn't," I said. "I'll be there in thirty minutes."

"Very well. I'll expect you."

I strapped on my shoulder holster, checked the gun, and put it on. I was just getting into my coat when the phone rang. I picked it up.

"Milo," he said, "this is George Henderson."

"Hi, George. Where are you?"

"I'm home. No trouble."

"Okay. I'll see you—at the usual place. Probably shortly after lunchtime."

"Okay." He hung up.

It took me less than a half hour to get to Westwood. I parked in front of the building and went in. Mrs. Masters opened the door.

"Very prompt, Mr. March," she said. "I like that in people. Come in."

I stepped inside and waited for her to sit down. She stopped just before she reached a chair. "Young man, do I smell alcohol on your breath?"

"I imagine so, Mrs. Masters," I said with a smile. "I take a bit of it for my neuritis. I find that it helps more than what the doctors give me."

"Is that so?" she asked. For the first time I saw a twinkle in her eyes. "I have a bit of neuritis myself. Would you like to join me in a bit of medicine, Mr. March?"

"I'd be happy to, Mrs. Masters," I said gravely.

"Will bourbon serve the purpose?"

"Like manna from heaven."

"I'll be right back," she said, and hurried out. She was soon back with two glasses of bourbon—and I mean glasses, not shots. I wondered why I was suddenly running into women who seemed determined to drink me under the table.

"Here we are," she said, putting the two glasses on the coffee table between the couch and the chair. She sat down. "It does give relief to take a nip now and again."

I sat down on the couch and picked up the glass. "To your good health, Mrs. Masters."

"And to yours, Mr. March." It was beginning to sound like a song in a musical comedy.

We drank. I noticed that she finished a good half of hers. "That's good bourbon," I said.

"Only the best. That was one of the few things that Harry taught me. Have you met the stripper, Mr. March?"

"Miss LaSalle? Yes, I've met her. She's pretty good at tossing down a drink herself."

"I hear that she's good in other departments as well."

"I wouldn't know about that," I said.

"A gentleman, too," she remarked. "Well, that's one thing Harry wasn't. Sometimes he'd come home while I was still up. He'd have a couple or three drinks and then he'd start telling me how great she was. I never knew whether it was true or whether he did it to make himself look better. Either way, it made no difference, so I'd let him talk. Finish your drink, Mr. March, and you can look through his room."

I picked up the glass and downed the bourbon. It made my eyes blink a little, but I managed it. Then I stood up.

"This way," she said, and walked toward the rear of the apartment. I followed her until we came to a closed door.

"This was Harry's room. I haven't even seen the inside of it in more than ten years except for the other day." She opened the door. "Help yourself, Mr. March. When you've finished, I'd like to ask your advice about something."

I nodded and went in, closing the door behind me. I stood still and looked around the room. It was neat, obviously used for little more than sleeping. There were two paintings on the wall—nudes. There was the bed, two chairs, two lamps, a TV, and a fairly large desk. One wall was all closets. I opened the doors and there were dozens of suits, slacks, and sport jackets. Also, inside the closets, there were two dressers filled with shirts, underwear, and socks. I closed the doors and went over to the desk.

There was a small bookcase next to it, but there wasn't a single book, nothing but copies of the *Wall Street Journal* and several right-wing magazines. I sat down in front of the desk. There was a small, neat pile of papers on top. I went through them. There wasn't much—a few personal bills, most of them marked paid; a notice to renew his subscription to the *Wall Street Journal;* a letter from a Congressman thanking him for his suggestions; a form letter from someone in the John Birch Society; and three or four circulars.

I turned my attention to the top drawer. It looked a little more promising. First, there was a calendar memo pad. None of the pages had been torn out, and there were notes or scribblings on them. I began to leaf through it.

There were a number of notations that didn't make sense— probably some sort of private code he'd worked out. I imagined that it could be easily broken, but was probably not too important. There were several pages of doodling. Nearly all of them included dollar signs. Some had the initials S.L. That was probably Sherry. He even put dollar signs around her. There were other pages with what looked like a headstone in a cemetery, but the only thing on the stone was a big dollar sign. On one page there was just the name "Gino," followed by a phone number. I copied that down. Another page had the figure "15" surrounded by dollar signs. Out of curiosity, I counted them. There were six. I wondered if that meant fifteen million dollars. On the page for the day of the fire there was a small + in the middle of the sheet. Below that, near the bottom of the page, there was an = sign. The next page, and the rest of the pad, was blank.

I put it on top of the desk and looked through the rest of the drawer. There were several credit cards and his personal checkbook. I went through it. In two months his balance had gone from more than $700,000 to less than $12,000. Most of the checks had been drawn to cash. The others had been for small amounts. On one check stub he had written a number on the margin. It had no relationship to his balance, but it could have been a phone number. I copied that down in my book too and added the checkbook to the pile on top of the desk.

There wasn't much else that interested me. Other drawers revealed a number of paid bills, a bundle of stocks, some government bonds, two pieces of jewelry, and, underneath some paid bills, an envelope with a thousand dollars in it.

That was about the extent of my findings. I picked up the calendar and the checkbook and carried them with me back into the living room. Mrs. Masters was sitting where I'd left her, but she had a fresh drink in front of her. She had also refilled my glass.

"Mrs. Masters," I said, "there are two things I'd like to take with me. I will give you a receipt for them and will return them later."

"What are they?"

"A calendar memo pad and Mr. Masters's personal checkbook."

"Take them," she said, waving her hand. "You don't have to bring them back. I'd just have the maid throw them out."

"I think you'd also better look through his desk," I told her. "There are several shares of stocks and bonds, two pieces of jewelry which might be worth something, and a thousand dollars in cash."

"Is there, now? Well, I'll go in and get those. Did you find anything you wanted?"

"I'm not sure. There are some curious things, but I want to study them further."

"I do hope you're wrong in your theory that Harry was murdered. It's such a grubby way to die." She took another drink and sighed. "Now, may I ask your advice, Mr. March?"

"Of course. I'll be glad to help you—if I can."

"The stripper," she said, "has finally made the approach to sell me the stock she owns. Her attorney got in touch with my attorney. She wants eight million dollars for the fifty-one percent. My attorney says that it's a very good price because the corporation is worth at least forty million and there would be no problem in raising eight million from the banks. She wants it in cash. What do you think I should do?"

I was surprised. Sherry had told me she should be able to get ten million for the stock, and now she was offering it for eight. To me, that meant one of two things. Either she wanted to get the money and leave as soon as possible, or she knew something about the value of the stock that no one else yet knew.

"What does your attorney say?"

"He thinks I should buy it at once before she offers it to other people. He says there's no doubt about the worth of the company."

"Do you want to buy the stock?"

"I guess so," she said slowly. "It would be nice to have the additional money, but I suspect I might want it to prove that I can run the business as well as Harry did. Her stock would give me seventy-six percent. What do you think, Mr. March?"

I took a deep breath. "If I were you, Mrs. Masters, I'd wait for a while. Stall her for a few days. You should be able to do that."

"Why?"

I decided to take a chance with her. "I don't have proof at the moment, but I have reason to believe that the company is not in as good condition as it seems to be. I expect to know definitely within a very few days. I'll let you know then."

She was silent for a minute. "All right, Mr. March. I respect your judgment and I'll take your advice without asking any other questions right now."

I finished my drink and stood up. "I'll be in touch with you as soon as I know anything. If you should want to call me anytime, I'm at the Continental Hotel. And thank you."

"Thank *you*," she said with a dry smile. "I wouldn't want to start my business career by losing eight million dollars."

I went back to the hotel, took the photograph of Masters out of the envelope, and put the calendar and checkbook in. I had the clerk put the envelope in the hotel safe. It was still early, so I decided to stop in to see Lieutenant Whitmore on my way downtown.

He was in his office, surrounded by papers as usual. There was a scowl on his face. It was still there when he looked at me.

"What do you want, March?"

"I just stopped in to bask in your sunny smile and see how things are going."

"You can see how they're going," he said, waving at the papers on his desk. "When things happen, they do it in bunches. There's enough work for the whole department just with the mess from the riot. Now I got a murder here in Hollywood that's driving us batty. There's no reason for it and there are no leads."

"Who was killed?" I asked idly.

"A little forger named Jimmy Altman. He was one of the best forgers in the country, but he liked his booze too well. Anyone wanted a good job out of him, they had to keep him sober until he finished it. That meant watching him every minute of the day and night. Most of the time he made enough money to keep going by forging driving licenses, credit cards—things like that. He was a mild little guy and never had any beefs with anyone. Anyway, somebody killed him the morning after the fires in the southeast."

"Any connection?" I asked.

He shook his head. "Between a forger and a race riot? How could there be? They didn't need any forged papers."

"Somebody killed him," I pointed out, but I was starting to lose interest. "Where'd it happen?"

"He lived in an old hotel on Hollywood Boulevard near Western—the Boulevard Hotel. Nobody saw him for several days. They were beginning to worry about him. Then that morning the man in the next room heard what he thought was a shot. He looked out and saw two men running down the stairs. The clerk came up and they found Jimmy had been shot."

"But you had witnesses?"

"Three of them, to be exact." He laughed. "You know, for a moment I thought we had two men we both know. The descriptions fit Benetto and Cabacchi exactly. But when we pulled them in, they both had alibis and the witnesses couldn't identify them. It's too bad."

SEVEN

Maybe Whitmore was wrong. I was suddenly interested again. And maybe it wasn't too bad at all. I could see a lot of interesting possibilities. If the Lieutenant's description of the forger was correct, I could think of no reason why Benetto and Cabacchi would have anything to do with him. They were simply muscle hoods; his traffic must have been with more sophisticated criminals. But suppose they had killed him. Why? Because a .38 will brush away a lot of footprints?

"Well," I said, "I'd better run along. I wish you luck on all your cases—especially the ones I'm interested in. I'll be seeing you, Lieutenant."

"Sure. Let me know next time and I'll have the tea on. Walk softly down the hall; some of the boys may be asleep."

"I thought they always were." I smiled at him and left.

My next stop was the bar over on the southeast side. George and some of his friends were there. George looked all right, but his face was drawn and his left arm was in a sling. I went over to join them, motioning to the bartender to give all of us a drink.

"How are you feeling?" I asked George.

"Great, just great. But don't slap me on the shoulder. I feel like being segregated just a mite."

"Turncoat," I said. "Did you find out what color your blood was when you were shot?"

"Red. Bright red. Maybe I'm an Indian instead of a black man."

"Okay, Chief Big Target, but maybe you better stay close to the reservation and help the squaws until you learn not to mess around with those palefaces who carry heap big lightning in their fists."

All of them laughed, including George.

"Don't mess around with me, white boy, or I won't give you the top secret information we collected for you."

"Sorry about that, Chief," I said. "I didn't know that the Pony Express had arrived. What's the latest?"

"We remembered something and we nosed around a bit and came up with a question for you."

"What do you think this is, the Quiz Kid hour?* Okay, I'll bite. What's the question?"

"What happened to the clean-up man?"

I stared at him blankly. "The clean-up man? What clean-up man?"

George shook his head. "Never answer a question with a question—first rule of communication. We mean the clean-up man in the Belters Building."

"Hell, I didn't even know that they had one. What about him?"

"He was a white cat, maybe in his early sixties. A wino, toothless. Maybe he hocked his teeth for a jug. He was always bragging about the great jockeys he used to know. They had some colored women who cleaned the whole building every

---

* *Quiz Kids* was a game show featuring children, broadcast on both radio (1940–1953) and TV (1949–1953).

night, but this old man was hired just to keep the Belters offices clean."

"Never heard of him," I said. "I never knew there was such a guy. Why the hell didn't anyone mention him before?"

George was grinning at me. "I don't know, boss man. Maybe because nobody knew about him except old man Masters, that brother-in-law of his, and us poor black folk down here. The old man and his brother-in-law are dead, and you didn't have much communication with us black people—not, at least, until recently, when you met up with some of our elite."

"Okay, okay," I said. "Let's stop the game. Tell me what the hell you're talking about."

"We don't exactly know, Milo," George said. "Old man Masters brought this cat down here about two weeks ago, something like that. Got him a place in a rooming house near here and turned him loose in the building. The guy immediately started getting fried on muscatel and stayed that way. He was the one who told everyone what his job was."

"Was Masters known for doing things like that?"

"I don't think so. Nobody down here ever saw much of him. He'd just come and go. He certainly wasn't known for his charity. And the local people who worked for him, like the women who cleaned the building and Bob Summers, got paid less than they would have gotten on a similar job almost anywhere in the city."

"So why did Masters bring this guy down here?" I asked. I was talking more to myself than to them. "How big a man was he?"

"He was pretty tall, but scrawny. Probably from too much wine and not enough food."

"Know what his name was?"

"He never told anybody. He was friendly, but he never said his name."

"All right. What was this question about what happened to him?"

"Just that," George said. "This morning, when I got out of the hospital, we were sitting around talking, and suddenly we remembered about him and that we hadn't seen him since the fire. We went around to the rooming house. He hasn't been there since the day of the fire. We went to see the man who runs the liquor store. It's not open or repaired. We saw him at home. But he hasn't seen the man since that day. So we came up with a question which we couldn't answer."

"So you throw it in my lap," I said. Then I smiled at them. "Thanks. I think I may know who the man was, but I'll have to do a little checking. And if he's who I think he is, it may be very important. I think I can find out by sometime tomorrow." I glanced at my watch. It was only a little after twelve. "Where's the nearest phone booth?"

"There's one right back there." George pointed toward the rear of the bar.

I squinted and could finally see it was a real booth. I got change from the bartender and put in a station-to-station call to The Sewer in Reno.

The receiver was lifted after the second ring. "Crooked Ted's," he said.

"This is Milo March. I'm the gin-and-grapefruit with the curious questions."

"How could I forget you?" he asked. "I always remember the drunks who come in here. Where are you?"

"Los Angeles. In another sewer. Remember the guy you told me about who used to be a trainer of racehorses?"

"Freddie? Sure."

"Will you do me a favor? You told me that Harry Masters said he was going to send Freddie back to Cleveland to see his family. See if you can find out if he did. If necessary, try to find out the name of his family and phone them to see if he arrived. I'll send you the money for anything you spend. If Freddie isn't in Ohio and they don't know where he is, see if anybody knows if he left Reno with Harry Masters. I'll call you tomorrow to see what luck you had."

"Okay," he said. "I'll run it down, Dr. Sherlock. Call me about this time tomorrow. I ought to have something. Don't bother to send me any money. Just buy me a drink."

"I'll buy you one now and send you the money."

"I'll choke it down."

"Thanks," I said. "I'll call you." I hung up and went back to the bar.

"Give us another round, bartender. Count yourself in."

"You see how it is?" George asked his friends. "These white boys try to come around and corrupt us by getting us to drink too much. Then they can look at us down their long white noses and say, 'Look at that colored boy! All he does is sit around and get drunk. No wonder he don't get nowhere in the world.' "

"Sure," I said easily. "I got another way of looking at it. You encourage us white cats to come around and buy you drinks until we finally go broke and have to take a job as a clean-up man or maybe sweeping the streets. Then you look down that short black nose and say, 'Look at that honky! Mean and shiftless, can't support himself or his folks. But I will say one thing for them honkies. They got two things going for them. They can really dance. Man, they got rhythm. They're born with it. And they're sexy. That's why we don't like them foolin' around with our women. They're too lazy to work, so they spend all their time with dancing and sex.' That's my side of the story."

This really broke them up. I finished my drink and shoved money across to the bartender. "My old grandfather," I said, "taught me three things: Never say no to a drink or a woman, and always leave them laughing. I'll see you tomorrow, but tell the bartender to turn on some lights so I can find you." I walked out.

Everyone at the Belters office would probably be at lunch, so I decided I'd go over later. I drove to Hollywood to my favorite bar, went in, and ordered a dry martini, some scrambled eggs, and toast. When Bo got a chance, he came back to where I sat.

"How's it going?" he asked.

"I'm not sure," I answered, "but I think pretty good. Listen, I just heard that a fellow named Jimmy Altman was killed in the Boulevard Hotel the day after the riot. Did you know him?"

"Not well, but I knew him. He'd come in here once in a while and have a few drinks. He liked his juice."

"Do you know what he did?"

"Somebody told me he was a forger, but I don't know."

"What did he seem like?"

"A nice quiet little guy. Never bothered anyone. Held his booze pretty good, paid for his drinks, and never talked much. That was all."

"Hear any rumors about why he was killed?"

"Nothing but rumors. This street is like an old women's sewing circle. Some people thought that Jimmy must have squealed on someone and was paid off. Others swear that he never talked in his life. Some thought he did a forgery job for someone important and was killed so he couldn't say anything. There were more rumors than facts. Why do you want to know? You carry insurance on Jimmy?"

"No. But I think I know who killed him and I'd like to see them get it."

"Why?"

"Because I think it's tied in with what I'm working on."

"Okay, okay," he said. "I just asked." He walked away to serve a customer.

My scrambled eggs arrived and I enjoyed them. Afterwards, I ordered one more drink for dessert. The place was busy by then, and Bo was too.

I was sipping my drink and aware that someone had slipped onto the stool next to me, but I didn't look around. Bo showed up. The man ordered a drink and I heard him tell Bo to give me one. I still didn't look around, until my drink arrived. Then I lifted it, looked at him, and said, "Cheers."

"Good health," he said.

I knew that the fact he'd bought me a drink was a sign he wanted to talk to me, so I waited patiently.

"You a cop?" he asked finally.

"No," I said. "Are you?"

I knew that in California a cop was supposed to answer this truthfully if he was asked in a public place.

He laughed. "No. Want to see my ID?"

"No. I'll take your word for it."

"I heard you asking about Jimmy Altman," he said. "What's your racket?"

I decided to more or less level with him. "My racket is that I'm an insurance investigator. I'm working on a case I think is more or less related to his murder. I also think that Jimmy Altman was killed by two cheap punks, and it was completely unnecessary! I'd like to see them take the rap for it. I hate cheap punks."

"Did you know Jimmy Altman?"

"No. I heard about him. He must have been a nice guy, because even the cops say so."

"You know who hit him?"

"I think so. If you know anything about it, tell me why the witnesses didn't identify the two men they saw."

"The muscle was put on them. They were scared."

"Okay. I can believe that. But I say they're punks and they'd faint if anybody said boo to them. You may quote me if you like."

"You know them?"

"I know them. Have you seen them recently?"

He nodded.

"Then," I said, "you may have noticed that one of them has a messed-up face. I gave it to him."

"How do I know you did?"

"Ask him. I don't think he knows my name, but he can describe me, although some of the adjectives may be inaccurate. Ask him what kind of car I drive. It's a new black Cadillac and it's parked right in front of this place. You can look at it and you'll also see it's a rental car. Now, what's this all about?"

"I won't ask them," he said with a smile. "I earn my bread in a quieter way." He thought for a minute. "Jimmy was a nice guy. You're right about one thing. He shouldn't have been hit. You're right about something else. He was killed because of a job he did. I don't know what the job was and I don't want to know. But I do know that two men stayed with him all the time he was on it, then someone stayed with him until the morning he was killed. So you figured that part right."

"I thought so," I said. He was carrying the ball and I wasn't going to push him.

"I'll tell you what," he said. "You go down to the Farrell Hotel on Fifth Street—not right now. Say, late this afternoon. Maybe five or six. Go up to room two-fifteen. When the door is opened, ask for Al. He'll be the guy who opens the door. Tell him that Dean sent you. He'll give you some information that may help."

"Thanks."

"Don't mention it," he said. "I owed Jimmy a couple of favors for a long time. Good luck." He slipped off the stool and was gone.

Bo came over in a few minutes. "What was that all about?" he asked.

"The guy was trying to give me a tip on a horse. You know how those touts are.

I'll see you later." He knew I was lying and there was a hurt look on his face as I left.

I drove into the parking lot on Wilshire and went up to the Belters offices. I told the girl I wanted to see Mr. Jeffers again. A moment later I was on my way to his office.

He was still obviously nervous about seeing me, but he tried to smile as he invited me to sit next to his desk. "How are you, Mr. March?" he asked. His hands shuffled his papers. "How's your report coming along?"

"Fine," I said. "It should be finished before long. Has your new majority stockholder shown up yet to give you her thinking on the future of the corporation?"

"No. We haven't heard from her. She may still be upset about the death of Mr. Masters."

"I imagine so," I said dryly. "I assume, however, that things are still progressing, the wheels of industry spinning, even though the real master is no longer at the till?"

"Something like that," he said. "Almost all of us here are experienced in the affairs of the corporation, and we can carry on."

"A noble spirit, Mr. Jeffers. I'm sorry to interrupt such industry, but there are a couple more questions I would like to ask you."

"Certainly. If there is any way I can be of assistance, I'll be only too happy to do so."

"I was sure you'd feel that way. I'd like a little more information about the way new business was acquired. At the moment, I think I understand it was Mr. Masters's practice to find a building or a business he wanted to buy and then purchase it himself. Later he would resell it to his corporation. Is that correct?"

"Yes, it is."

"I'm curious about how this was handled. Did he pay cash for such properties, or did he arrange some sort of mortgage? I should imagine, since some of these properties were very valuable, a cash transaction would involve more than Mr. Masters could handle by himself."

"I was not intimate with Mr. Masters's personal finances, but I would think that he was personally worth enough to handle almost anything."

"As much as three or four million dollars?"

"Yes. Don't forget that Mr. Masters was in business for a good many years and always made money. I don't know whether he kept it all in banks or in stocks, but I should think his worth was considerable."

"All right. Tell me how it worked, say, on the last piece of property that was bought out in the Valley very recently. I believe it involved more than three million dollars."

"That is correct," he said. "The exact price was four million dollars. Mr. Masters bought it free and clear. He made an agreement with the corporation to sell it to us for that sum. We then went to one of our banks, presented the agreement, and asked them what sort of mortgage arrangement they would make with us. They appraised the building and land and offered to loan us three and one half million dollars the moment Mr. Masters transferred the title to us. Mr. Masters did so; we signed the papers with the bank; and they credited us with that amount of money. We then gave Mr. Masters a corporation check for four million dollars." He smiled intimately. "To tell you the truth, Mr. March, I always suspected he made a small profit on those deals, but he was only making it from himself, so there was nothing wrong."

Small profit, hell. As I saw that one transaction, Masters had bought the property with an option of fifty thousand dollars, then gotten three and a half million dollars covered by a mortgage. He had turned around and sold it to his corporation for four million dollars and received that much from them. They had taken out a three and a half million dollar mortgage with another bank. So, by my mathematics, Mr. Masters had made a profit of four million dollars on one deal, and two banks held mortgages worth seven million dollars without yet being aware of each other.

"I was wondering about that," I said. "It seemed to me that it was a most unusual business method, and I'm surprised that the banks went along with it."

"But Mr. Masters had been in business a long time. His credit and integrity were well known. He was recognized as one of the last individual tycoons, and he was respected. His word was his bond."

"I'm surprised that he didn't need more words by this time," I said, but I could see that he didn't get that. "Did he always do business this way?"

"I don't believe so. I think it only started about a year ago, when we began to speed up our expansion."

"I see. Well, it's all very interesting. Tell me, Mr. Jeffers, how often do you have an audit of the business?"

"Twice a year. I believe the next one is due in a week or two."

"Well, good luck," I said, and walked out without looking back.

Downstairs, I tried calling the number for Benetto that I'd found on Masters's memo pad, but there was no answer. Then I phoned Sherry. She answered on the third ring, still sounding half asleep.

"Hi, baby," I said, "this is Milo. Sorry I woke you up."

"That's all right, honey. You coming over?"

"No. I'll see you tonight. I'll catch you when the last show is over and we'll go out to dinner. I'll be at the bar when you come out."

"Okay, honey," she said.

I checked the time when I got out of the phone booth. It was too late to start going around to the banks and too early to go downtown to see Al. So I had to kill some time. I drove back over to Hollywood and stopped in at the bar. There were only three men there. I took a stool in the middle of the bar and ordered a gin and grapefruit juice when Bo came over.

"What was that all about today?" he asked when he brought the drink.

"Better off if you don't know," I said.

"Okay, if you want to be stuffy," he said. He reached back and took a quarter from the register. "Here. Play the jukebox and make yourself useful."

"You and your jukebox," I said scornfully. "Someday, when I get rich, I'm going to buy a bar just so I can put in a jukebox with nothing but blank records in it." I went over, put the quarter in, and punched the first numbers I saw. Then I went back to my drink and my thoughts.

The case was beginning to shape up, and I was starting to feel the tense elation I always got when it reached this point. There were still problems ahead, but for the first time I felt that all the little pieces would fall into place. Most of the time I liked my job—at least, the last part of it. I had to deal with crumbs and cheap punks—no matter how much money they thought they could steal—and I liked to see them take a dive.

The way I pictured it at the moment, Mr. Big Business Masters had decided at some time that he wasn't satisfied with just going on making a million or so a year. He wanted to make a big score, not have to pay taxes on it, and go off to gambol on the green somewhere with a delicious broad. From then on, he would be on a sleigh ride (or maybe a slay ride), and he didn't care how the chips fell, as long as they dropped into his lap. He figured out a scheme where he could pluck several million dollars out of the air, and leave his corporation and several banks holding the bag for twice what he stole. Nice.

Also, he didn't stop to think that along the way he was going to have to kill three people—no, probably four—and he didn't much care. All he wanted was the loot and the sexy broad, and then to split. It was all very smart and very chic, and he'd be laughing somewhere and patting the broad on the bottom while the suckers were scrambling to put their lives, if there were any left, back together again. A nice guy and a nice broad.

All I had to do now was to sew it all together neatly so that he would take the full rap—he and all the people he had used or bought. Nice people he had used, not-so-nice people he had used with their complete consent. I'd still bet that he knew all the time that Sherry couldn't sell the stock, and he didn't care; she wouldn't know where he was, only a contact point. He wouldn't care about that either. He had plenty of money. She was a nice broad, but there were always plenty of nice broads when you had money. Then there were the sewer rats that you could buy who knew nothing.

Sure, all I had to do was sew it up—with even stitches. Just prove that he did it, how he did it, who helped him, where he was, and how to get him back to face the music. That was all. Nothing to it. I swore to myself under my breath. I felt like going out and getting drunk, but it wasn't that easy for me. Work first and then, when it was over, I'd be too tired and disgusted to get drunk. So to hell with it.

I had my drink and felt angry and badgered, and wanted some way to work it off. This always meant that I had to find some way of pushing certain people. It would give me a release and force things to a quicker ending.

Then I got an answer to the way I was feeling. It walked through the door. It was Gino Benetto, his face swollen and mottled, his eyes angry and discolored. He saw me and started walking stiff-legged. He'd seen too many Western movies. I watched him in the mirror back of the bar; he knew I was watching him. He went on to the end of the bar and sat down without looking directly at me. He ordered a screwdriver, which Bo served him.

I finished my drink and nodded at Bo. He came over.

"Give me a drink," I said, low enough not to be heard by anyone else, "and I want to buy a drink for the thing that just came in. I'm going to put money on the bar and go to the men's room. Make the drinks slowly and serve them just as I come out—his in front of him, mine next to him. Then go back and take the money out of what I put down. Put my change in front of where I was sitting and don't pay any attention to what's going on between us. He wouldn't like it if he knew anyone else saw what is going to happen to him."

"Okay," Bo said, "but don't get my place shot up."

"I won't," I said. "But just do what I'm telling you." I put a five-dollar bill on the bar, got up, and walked back to the men's room without looking at Benetto. I waited there for a couple of minutes. I didn't think he'd follow me, but I was ready if he did.

Finally I walked back slowly and as quietly as I could. I took my gun from the holster and held it close to my waist so no one else would see it. Bo was serving the drinks just as I arrived at the stool.

"It's on this gentleman," Bo said.

I slid onto the stool and had my gun in his belly, out of sight below the bar, before he could turn to look.

"Hello, Gino," I said. "Just sit like a little gentleman and have the drink I bought for you—unless you want to try for one on the house. If you do want to, go ahead. It'll probably make you feel better. Your lip won't hurt at all if you try."

EIGHT

His muscles tightened until it seemed he might burst out of his clothes, but he didn't look around, and the only move he made was to pick up the glass slowly. His hand was steady as he took a swallow. I knew that he considered throwing it in my face, but he knew I was aware of it and could pull the trigger faster than he could throw.

"I'm going to kill you," he said. His voice was so low I could barely hear him.

"You've got it all wrong, Gino," I said. "You're not going to kill me. You're not man enough. I'm going to kill you. But not directly. That would be easy. I'm going to make sure you get sent up for murder. I'm going to hang one on you, baby, that's going to stick."

He made a rude suggestion.

I laughed. "Take a walk, baby," I said. I stood up and stepped back so he could leave. The gun wasn't up against him now, but he knew it was still trained on him. "Just walk out and don't come back. If you're smart, you'll keep on walking until you're out of town."

"I'll get you," he said.

"You're repeating yourself, Gino. Just start walking. I don't want to get blood all over the nice floor in here. Move."

He took one step, stopped, and looked directly at me for

the first time. His eyes shone as if someone had put shellac over them. "What's your racket? You ain't no cop. Why are you digging around in things that ain't any of your business? What are you, some kind of Boy Scout?"

"I tried for the Girl Scouts, but they wouldn't have me," I said. "Just say that I've got an itch to see them put you in a little room and throw the key away. And I'm the guy who's going to do it to you. Now, on your way, crumb."

He stared at me for another second. He wanted to make a try for me, but he didn't have the guts. He turned and walked on stiff legs to the door and out of sight. I put my gun away and went back to my drink.

"Don't do that again," Bo said, coming up to me. "You'll give me a nervous breakdown. I thought the joint was going to be sprayed with bullets any minute."

"Not by him. He doesn't have the nerve."

"Maybe not, but you know he's probably going to be waiting for you outside."

"Maybe. But he still won't have the nerve. Don't worry. I wouldn't hurt a glass of your boozery."

"Yeah, but he would," Bo said gloomily.

I had another drink and then decided it was time to go. I used the back door, stopping as I reached the street to look around. Gino wasn't in sight. He was probably parked around the corner, waiting for me to come out the front door. I got into my car and took off, up Gramercy.

I made one stop at Western Union, where I sent a sixty-cent money order to Teddie at The Sewer in Reno. Then I drove downtown and parked near the Farrell Hotel. It was a sleazy-looking place. The clerk paid no attention as I walked past him and up the stairs. I found room 215 and knocked on the door.

The door opened. A tall, gaunt man looked out.

"Are you Al?" I asked.

He nodded.

"Dean sent me," I told him. He opened the door wider and I stepped inside. It was just another cheap room. There was a bed and one chair and a beat-up dresser. It didn't look as if anyone was living there. I guessed that it was merely rented for meetings like this one. The man sat on the bed and I took the chair. He didn't look too happy about being there with me.

"I was told that you could give me some information about Jimmy Altman. Did you know him?"

"Yes," he said reluctantly. "We weren't friends, but I knew him. Sometimes he bought certain kinds of paper from me."

"For his work?"

"I suppose so. I never asked."

"You knew what kind of work he did?"

"I didn't exactly know. I guessed what it was, and I sometimes heard rumors. I knew the kind of work he once did. His reputation was big at one time, you understand. He was a great artist. Recently he bought very little stock from me, and what he did buy was very ordinary."

"How about just before he was killed?"

He sighed. "Then he bought some better papers and other supplies he hadn't used much recently. It wasn't so unusual an order, either in kind or size, but the circumstances were different."

"In what way?"

"Well, he used to come down to see me. I have a little shop not far from here. You must understand that everything I sell is completely legal. How it's used after I sell it may be against the law, but I'm not responsible. It's like silver. Silver is legal; to make coins from the silver is illegal."

"I understand," I said. "I have no intention of involving you in any way. What did he do this time that was different than other times?"

"He phoned me and told me what he wanted and said that a man named Gino would pick it up and pay me. He was also sober, which was most unusual in recent years."

"Did this Gino come?"

"Yes. He, too, was unusual. He was not the type of person to be a friend of Jimmy's. He picked up the material and paid for it from a large roll of bills. Jimmy never had money like that. Usually he had to charge what he bought and then he'd pay me for it a few days later. He always did pay, too."

"You say that the man who came was not the type to be Jimmy's friend. Why?"

"Jimmy was educated and had an appreciation of fine things. He loved art, for example. Before he started drinking so much, he would spend hours in galleries and museums. I always thought Jimmy would have been an artist if he hadn't discovered a way to make more money with his talent. The man who came was as far from that sort of life as you could imagine. He was uneducated and brutal. I noticed that he carried a gun. Jimmy did break laws, perhaps, but he never owned a gun and wouldn't have known how to use one if he had."

"Was he buying the results of Jimmy's work, do you think?"

"He must have been."

"Would you be able to identify the man if you saw him again?" I asked.

He hesitated. "I suppose I would, but I'd rather not be put in that position."

"Why? If your work is legal, it wouldn't make trouble for you."

"I wasn't thinking about the police," he said slowly. "It was the man who came here. I've seen men like that before. Frankly, I'm afraid of him."

"I understand," I said.

I left the room and went back to my car. I drove straight back to my hotel. There was no sign of Gino and Joe. I stopped at the desk, but there were no messages, so I went on up to the room.

It was too late to see most of the people I still had to visit, and quite a few hours before I was due to show up at The Bodies to pick up Sherry. I phoned room service and asked them to send up a bucket of ice and a club sandwich. I noticed that my laundry and dry cleaning had been delivered while I was out. By the time I had put it away, the waiter arrived. I signed the check and waved him away.

As soon as he was gone, I undressed, made a drink, and leaned back on the bed with enjoyment. After the first drink, I made a second one and started nibbling on the sandwich. I also lit a cigarette. Some people get upset by the fact that I like to drink, eat, and smoke at more or less the same time.

The sandwich, the drink, and the cigarette were all finished, so I made another drink, lit another cigarette, and got into a more comfortable position. It was time I did some more homework.

What sort of person was Harry Masters? I thought I had a good idea of him. He was a man with a drive for power. Even his drive for money was a part of it. His gambling was also a part. If he'd ever had a losing streak, he'd probably have stopped gambling. The young women he bought were part of it. It made him feel powerful to control them and to be seen with them in public. From what his wife and Kitty Harris had said, I doubted that he had much of a sex drive; it was ownership and manipulation and display that he really needed.

His business history as I'd figured it out also fit the pattern. As large as his company had grown, it was still a one-man operation. His employees were merely drudges who did what he told them, and did it in the way he ordered. But he had reached a point where, if he grew much more, he couldn't continue in that fashion. A much bigger corporation would eventually have to have outside stockholders, and they would undoubtedly question many of the things he did. Rather than permit that, I suspected, he would have destroyed what he'd built.

Many people, I'm sure, would have called him an immoral man. He wasn't. He was an amoral man. It wasn't that he flaunted moral values; they had no meaning for him. Everything was ego-centered with him, and he knew no other way to function—even the little games he played buying a business and then turning it over to his own corporation at a slight profit. I doubted that he needed that extra money, but if he had needed cash he could have simply taken it from the corporation. He controlled it. The whole operation had been a game.

I was sure that he was a smart businessman. He must have been aware that he couldn't get any larger without giving up his method of running everything. I was sure he would never have agreed to that. He could have hired someone to run the business and retired with a good income. Or he could have sold the business and invested his money where it would give him retirement money. I was certain he would never have agreed to that either.

So, I thought, he was left with only one choice—the one I believed he had taken. He would grab all the money he could from the company, leaving it crippled or destroyed, and disappear. If he had enough money, he could probably start over and run his new business the way he liked in another country. If he had covered his tracks well enough, he might never be found.

To pull off such a plan he would need help. That might partly explain Sherry and would explain Benetto and Cabacchi. They would be weak links in the chain, especially the two men. If Masters was as smart as I thought he was, he'd probably have devised a method of paying them a fairly large sum of money in installments over a period of time. If they did any talking, the payments would stop, which would keep them on his side for a while. By that time he might be living anywhere under a third or fourth name. There was a possibility of getting the two gangsters into a talking mood, but only if I could try to pin so much on them that they would get frightened enough to talk.

It meant I still had a lot of work to do, and not too much time to do it in. With that pleasant thought, I put out my cigarette and went to sleep.

It was ten o'clock when I woke up, about the time I had in mind. I sat up and poured myself a drink. I sipped it slowly while the sleep faded from my mind, before I got up and dressed. Downstairs an attendant brought my car. I drove away, watching the rearview mirror, but there was no sign of anyone following. I drove straight to The Bodies.

The show was already on when I entered, so I went to the bar and ordered a bourbon. I made it last throughout the show without even looking at the girls.

"Hello, honey," Sherry said a few minutes later. "You ready?"

I finished my bourbon and turned to look at her. She was as beautiful as always.

"Ready," I said, sliding off the stool.

This time we went to a different restaurant. It was also small and intimate, and the food was excellent. We were out of there relatively early. I drove her home and parked in front of the building.

"Coming up, honey?" she asked.

"Sure."

Upstairs, we went through the same routine. She excused herself to get into something comfortable and came back in the same style nightgown, only in a different color. Then we went into the kitchen to make drinks, but this time I ducked the blockbuster and had straight brandy. We carried them back to the living room.

"This morning," I said, "I noticed there were several maps on the stand next to your bed. Is that how you read yourself to sleep at night?"

"No, honey," she said, laughing. "I don't have to read myself to sleep. I told you my agent has a job for me in Paris. Those are maps of all the places I've always wanted to see— Paris, Rome, places like that."

"It must be exciting to look forward to seeing places you've always wanted to visit. When do you go to Paris for the job?"

"In about two weeks. I can hardly wait."

"I'll bet. What about Rome? Are you going there, too?"

"My agent thinks he can get me in a club there. He hasn't made a definite deal with them because he thinks I'll get a long engagement in Paris. The contract is for four weeks, but they have the option to extend it. He says they'll love me in Paris."

"I'm sure they will," I said. "Maybe I'll come over and visit you while you're there."

"Would you, honey? That would be wonderful. We'd have a ball."

I had to give her an A for effort. She managed to make it sound as if she couldn't wait for me. She went on chattering about the idea of working in Paris, and I let her wander. She was only interrupted by the emptiness of her glass. She brought back two drinks from the kitchen.

"Where was I, honey?" she asked.

"In Paris," I said. "Don't you have to sell your stock before you go?"

"No, I've offered it for sale, but if it isn't sold before I have to leave, I'll let my attorney handle it. He can finish the deal and put the money where I'll get an income from it."

The phone rang. She frowned and went over to answer it. There was a sudden tightening of her face and a movement of her head that made me suspect I was involved in the call in some way. Maybe I was wrong, but the impression was distinct.

"No," she said. There was a new, hard quality to her voice. She listened for a minute more. "No," she said again, "I don't care what you want. You'll wait until I tell you that it's all right. That was made perfectly clear to you."

She hung up and came back to her chair.

"Sorry, honey," she said. "That's some jerk who keeps trying to come up and see me. I told him over and over again that if I want to see him I'll tell him it's okay, but until then to leave me alone."

I didn't believe her, but I played it her way. "Who can blame him?" I said. "You're a beautiful broad."

"You're sweet," she said. "You always say the nicest things. I don't really believe you mean it, but I like to hear you talk anyway."

"I mean it," I told her.

Then we went back to the subject of her career and what she was going to do in Paris. I listened to her opinions, smiling and nodding my head, through several more drinks. Then we went back to the script. She stood up, thrust out her chest, and demanded to know why we didn't make love. I finished my drink and followed her into the bedroom. The rest of it was also pre-programmed. But don't get me wrong. It was great. And it ended the same way as it had the night before—except that I didn't go to sleep at once.

I'd figured out one thing about her. She probably didn't even know what happened. She kept pulling on those French seventy-fives all day and all night, then had three or four fast ones when she got home, and by that time she was so far out all she needed was one more little push—which she got in bed—before she passed out. She was already snoring gently and there was no reaction when I pushed her arm.

The light was still on in the living room, so I got up and walked over to the desk. I opened a couple of drawers and finally found her address book. I started to look through it.

Finally I found one item I was looking for, under G for Gino—a phone number, and it was the same one that Masters had written on his calendar pad. I glanced through the rest of the book, but didn't find anything more of interest. The only number she had for Masters was a local one, probably his office.

I inspected the rest of the desk, but didn't find anything of interest. I didn't really expect to. One slip was all you could hope to find at a time. I went back to bed and to sleep.

This time I was up very early. It wasn't quite seven o'clock when I opened my eyes, slid out of bed, and got dressed. She still hadn't moved and didn't show any signs of doing so. I left and went down to my car. Back at the hotel, I ordered some breakfast and a bucket of ice, and slipped into the shower. I was out just in time to let the waiter in. I signed the check and he left. I lingered over my coffee because I knew there wouldn't be anyone I could interview this early. Then the phone rang. I swallowed the last bite of scrambled eggs and picked up the receiver.

"Hello," I said.

"Milo, boy," a voice said, "how are you?" It was Martin Raymond in New York.

"I'm just fine," I said. "You were considerate enough to let me finish my eggs before you phoned. I appreciate that."

"Eggs at this time of day?"

"Martin," I said gently, "you're supposed to be an alert executive. You should know that there's a certain difference in time between New York and California. There's no one in any of the offices out here yet—unless it's a burglar. When they are in their offices, I'll be around. As a matter of fact, I'm working day and night." I hated to include Sherry in the work schedule, but in a way that's where she belonged.

"Sorry," he said. "I forgot the time difference. The board was delighted with your report to me. How are things going?"

"Things are going great—or were until you called. The minute they are greater I will send you word by the first dog sled out of here. Don't forget that this is a primitive country. They haven't even learned to keep the same time as Madison Avenue."

"I told you I'm sorry," he said stiffly. "I thought you'd like to hear the board's reaction. You will keep in touch?"

"By all means, even carrier pigeon. Thank you for calling, Martin. I really appreciate it." I put the receiver gently down on the hook.

I finished my coffee and felt a little better. After I'd shaved and dressed, I went downstairs and had my car brought around in front. No one was following as I drove down Sunset.

I parked near the bar and went in. George and his friends were there. I took a stool next to George and told the bartender to give all of us a drink.

"We were worried about you, baby," George said. "We thought maybe your two friends caught up with you."

"Not them. I caught up with one of them yesterday, though, and gave him a little extra push with a gun, so we'll probably have a showdown within the next few days. You want to come along and ride shotgun?"

"Not me, man. I'm a soul brother who believes in peace. You wouldn't want me to get messed up with them evil men, would you?" He paused a moment. "When do we leave?"

"I didn't say we were leaving," I answered with a smile. "Any more news about the clean-up man?"

"Not a word. It's like they shot him off for a moon landing."

I glanced at my watch. "Maybe I can get some word now." I checked to make sure I had enough change and then went back to the phone booth and put in my station-to-station call to The Sewer in Reno.

"Good morning," said a voice that was becoming familiar, "Crooked Ted's."

"Good morning, Teddie," I said, "this is Milo March."

He chuckled. "Got your telegram. I managed to choke one down."

"I knew you'd make it," I said. "Any news about Freddie?"

"I found his family in Cleveland. They haven't seen him or heard from him in years. Then I spoke to one of our cab drivers. He says that Freddie left with Masters that day—at least they boarded the plane together. He said that Freddie was wearing a new suit. I guess maybe he got drunk in Los Angeles and never made it east of there. Probably cashed in his ticket and bought wine with it."

"Yeah, I guess he got drunk," I said. "Thanks, Ted. I'll see you soon."

I hung up and went back to the bar. George looked at me as I sat down.

"I found out who he was," I said. "His name was Freddie Freeman. He used to train racehorses, but lately all he's done is ride the muscatel. He thought some nice guy was going to put him on a plane in Los Angeles so he could go to Cleveland and visit his folks."

"Maybe he went."

I shook my head. "You can bet he took a longer trip than that. He was one of those three ... *things* they found in the Belters Building ashes."

"Damn," George said.

"I'll join in that prayer," I told him. I finished my drink. "I'll see you cats around." Then I got up and left.

I parked near the Belters office on Wilshire and went up to see Frank Jeffers. He wasn't glad to see me, but he pretended to be.

"Good morning, Mr. March," he said. "What can I do for you today?"

"Not much," I admitted. "I'd like the names and addresses of the banks that Belters does business with. I don't mean the special account. The others."

"Certainly." He pulled over a memo pad and scribbled on it. He tore off the sheet and handed it to me.

"By the way, do you know if Mr. Masters had more than one personal account?"

"I don't know. I never heard of another." He was frowning. "Is there anything wrong, Mr. March?"

"Nothing at all, Mr. Jeffers. Everything is just peachy."

Outside, I looked at the sheet. There were four banks listed on it. They were all in the neighborhood. I left my car in the lot and walked to the first one. I was ushered into one of those open pens to see the manager, told him who and what I was, and showed him my identification.

"What can I do for you, Mr. March?" he asked.

"I'm sure you know about the death of Mr. Masters in the fire that recently destroyed one of his buildings?"

"Oh, yes. That was a great tragedy. I'm sure that Mr. Masters will be greatly missed by the business community."

"Yeah," I said. "Had Mr. Masters done business with you long?"

"Ten years with the branch. And he had been with one of our other branches for fifteen years before that. I imagine that we will continue to do business with the corporation, but it won't be the same as when Mr. Masters was there."

"I expect not. I believe that you hold a mortgage on some property that the corporation recently acquired out in the Valley?"

"That is correct. An excellent piece of property. He paid only four million dollars for it. When our appraisers looked it over, we were happy to give him three and a half million dollars and take a mortgage. That property will double in value in the next ten years."

"That must be a comforting thought," I said. "I understand that Mr. Masters first bought that property personally and then sold it to his corporation. Isn't that a bit unusual?"

"It is unusual, but there's nothing wrong with it. In the case of a man with the business acumen of Mr. Masters, it was undoubtedly an advantage."

"How's that?"

"He'd wander around until he found something he wanted and then he'd go in and buy it—off the street, as it were. Many times, I'm sure, if it had been known that a big corporation wanted the property, the price might well have gone up slightly."

"I suppose so. Is that the only mortgage you hold on the property of the corporation?"

He smiled. "No, we held a mortgage on the building that was burned down. It was almost paid off, and I imagine the insurance will adequately take care of the balance."

"Do you know if other banks also hold mortgages on property purchased by the corporation?"

"I don't personally know of any, but I should imagine that there are several mortgages. The corporation has been expanding rapidly, especially during the last year."

"Would you say too rapidly, in your estimation?"

He pursed his lips. "No, I wouldn't. It's true that expansion has often left them with a cash reserve lower than we would normally recommend, but over the years they have demonstrated an ability to operate without getting into difficulties. Mr. Masters's track record is very good."

"I was thinking that he was a good runner myself," I said. "Well, thank you for your assistance."

"That's what I'm here for," he said. "Be glad to help you anytime, Mr. March." We shook hands and I left.

I visited the other three banks and discovered that they held mortgages ranging from three to five million dollars. I checked back with the bank I had first visited a few days earlier. They still had their three and a half million dollar mortgage on the property in the Valley. Mortgage payments, they reported, had been made promptly.

Finally I found a bar on one of the side streets in the neighborhood. I went in and had a dry martini while I went over the notes I had made. According to the various bank managers. Masters had received at least seventeen million dollars. In one specific case I knew he had gotten four million, and there were two mortgages for three and a half million each on the same property. I suspected that this was true of the other properties bought within a period of less than one year.

No matter how I added it up, it came to about the same figure. Harry Masters had managed to put seventeen million in his pocket. The corporation and/or his estate was stuck with a tab of thirty-four million dollars plus what they owed on previous mortgages and commercial loans. In other words, it looked like they owed more than they were worth on paper. I'd still have to run down the rest of the operations and find out where the money had gone, but at least I had a pretty clear picture of how it had been done.

I went back to the Belters offices and asked to see Miss Lester, Masters's last secretary. She was still there.

"How are things going?" I asked her.

She shrugged. "I haven't been fired and no one has given me anything to do, so I just sit at my desk and read until they get around to me."

"How about having lunch with me?"

"I'd love to," she said. "Just give me three minutes." She disappeared. I didn't have long to wait. She was back promptly. I took her to the place where I'd had a drink. It turned out to be a good choice. We talked about a variety of things during lunch without once mentioning the Belters corporation. Then I walked her back to her office building.

"Well, thank you, Mr. March," she said, putting out her hand.

"Not so fast," I told her. "I'm coming up with you. I want some more help from you."

She laughed. "So it wasn't just my fatal charm."

"The lunch was your charm, but now it's business hours again."

We went upstairs and I followed her into her office.

"What can I do for you, Mr. March?"

"I know about one personal bank account which Mr. Masters had, but I'm sure he had others. Would you know anything about those?"

"No. I never had anything to do with his personal finances."

"I think he might have kept some record of other accounts here in his office. Are you sure that you never ran across them?"

"Positive," she said. She hesitated a moment. "Mr. Masters did have one drawer in his desk which was always locked.

I've never seen into that drawer, but he might have kept financial information there."

"Where was the key kept?"

"Mr. Masters carried his with him." She hesitated again, this time a little longer. "There is one other key. I have it, but Mr. Masters gave me strict orders never to use it unless he told me to do so."

"Would you let me look through the drawer? You can stand by to see that I don't purloin anything."

"I don't know," she said slowly. "I guess there isn't anyone to ask either. And I suppose you do have sort of a right. Okay, Mr. March." She opened a drawer in her desk and took out a small key. "Come on, before I lose my nerve."

Masters's private office was next to hers. She opened the door and we went inside, closing the door behind us. It was a huge room with wall-to-wall carpeting, a large desk, a couple of filing cabinets, and a few simple pieces of furniture. She marched across to the desk and unlocked the center drawer.

"There," she said. She sounded nervous. "But please hurry, Mr. March. I wouldn't want to be found in here. I don't know how I would explain it."

"I doubt if anyone will come in," I said, "but if they do, I'll handle it." I moved over and sat down in Masters's chair. I opened the drawer.

There were a number of papers in it, plus a small notebook and two checkbooks. I picked up the notebook and looked in it. It contained a list of mortgages, with the amount and date due on payments. These were the ones on which he had to make personal payments. I noticed that there were two mortgages I didn't know about. And there were probably two other mortgages to match them on which the corporation was making payments to two different banks.

I turned to the checkbooks. They both were in the name of Harry Masters, but with a post-office box number. I looked through the stubs. Both were filled with large deposits and large withdrawals. There were smaller checks also, which must have been mortgage payments. I took out a slip of paper and jotted down the large deposits and the large withdrawals. The last withdrawal had been made the day of the fire. I also wrote down the names of the two banks.

Then I looked through the other papers. They mostly were concerned with information about various stocks on the New York market. There were a few letters from women, but the names were ones I didn't know, and none of the dates were recent.

I slipped my notes in my pocket and closed the drawer, then stood up and looked at her. "Okay, honey, you can lock it up."

She did so and we stepped outside. Nobody paid any attention to us as we entered her office. She was trembling when she sat at her desk and put the key back in the drawer.

"I don't know why I did that," she said. She looked up at me. "There's something going on here, isn't there?"

"Can you keep things to yourself?" I asked.

"I have to now, don't I? I went in and unlocked that drawer for you. I can't very well talk about anything without telling about that, too."

"I can't tell you very much now, but something has already

gone on here. You may lose your job, and I strongly suspect that everyone here will be looking for work. But don't even hint at that to anyone. It will only make them panic and maybe make things more difficult."

"I don't know what you're talking about," she said. "Wouldn't even know what to hint at."

"Good girl. Keep it that way."

"But it does have something to do with Mr. Masters's death, doesn't it?"

"In a way. That's only a small part of it. I promise you one thing—before I leave Los Angeles I'll buy you the best dinner in town and tell you as much as I can. But be sure you keep buttoned up."

She smiled. "I've seen enough movies to know what happens to people who talk too much."

"You've nothing to fear from me."

She took a deep breath. "You're wearing a gun."

"You've been peeking."

"When you bent over the desk, your jacket was unbuttoned and I saw it."

"I also have a license to carry that gun. Would you like to see it?"

She shook her head. "I believe you. I have to now."

"Don't worry about it, honey. You did the right thing. We'll have that dinner date soon. I'll call you."

I went downstairs and out to my car. After I'd gotten in behind the wheel and put the key in the ignition, I took the slip of paper with the noted withdrawals from my pocket. I'd been wrong before. Harry Masters had stolen at least twenty-two million dollars. That money, in cash, was somewhere around. It was either with a very much alive Harry Masters or with someone who had killed him to get it.

NINE

No matter how you looked at it, that was a lot of money. It hurt me just to think of that much money floating around the world. Only it probably wasn't floating, but was solidly anchored somewhere, so that no unauthorized person could get to it. The problem would be to find out where it was, and that couldn't be solved by sitting down and asking yourself where you'd go if you were twenty-two million dollars.

I went to the two banks I'd found listed in the book in Masters's desk. Each of them had a mortgage on property owned by Harry Masters. The payments had been made regularly. Yes, they knew that Masters was dead, but they were certain, based on their previous dealings, that the payments would be taken over by the estate or by the corporation. I also found another bank which held a mortgage on one of these same properties made out in the name of the corporation. I didn't find a fourth bank, but I was sure there was one.

I drove back to Hollywood and stopped to see Lieutenant Whitmore. He seemed just as harassed as ever when he looked up and scowled at me.

"Why don't you just move in?" he asked. "We must have a spare cot somewhere around here."

"It's your fascinating personality," I told him. "I want to ask you two questions."

"What?"

"Did you find any kind of physical clue to the identity of any one of the bodies in the fire? I mean other than measurements."

"Which fire? The Belters Building?"

"Yes."

"We found something, but it's not of much value. There was an old break in the right leg below the kneecap of one of them."

"Which body?"

"The one whose measurements matches those of Harry Masters. But it's not worth anything. There is no way of verifying that Masters had once sustained such a break."

"Mrs. Masters?"

"She didn't know about it, but said it could have happened before she met him. And she doesn't know who his doctor was at the time. What else?"

"That Altman murder at the Boulevard Hotel—do you think Benetto and Cabacchi did it?"

"I think so, but what I think doesn't mean a damn. The witnesses didn't identify them."

"Think they were threatened?"

"What do you suppose?" he demanded. "But how do you prove that?"

"Do you think they might change their testimony if the witnesses feel Benetto and Cabacchi are no longer in a position to carry through on the threats?"

"Probably. Why?"

"Maybe I can help. I'll let you know." I turned and left. I drove to the Casa Del Monte and went in.

Bo mixed a gin and grapefruit juice and brought it over to me. "How's it going?" he asked.

"Who knows?" I said shrugging. "Remember when I was in here talking with you about the murder of Jimmy Altman and there was a man who bought me a drink and talked to me for a while?"

He nodded. "That was Dean. I don't know his last name. He comes in here pretty regularly."

"I'd like to get in touch with him today if possible."

"He should be here in the next thirty minutes or so. That's the time he usually comes in."

"All right. I'll be back. Tell him I want to see him and, if he can, have him wait for me. Put his drinks on me and I'll pay when I get back."

"The way you're playing around with that Gino, I should make you pay for every drink in advance. But I'll tell him."

I finished my drink and left. On my way out I stopped at the public phone and called a newspaperman I knew. He was in.

"When did you get in town?" he asked.

"A few days ago, but I haven't had any time for fun and games. Look, you know Gino Benetto and Joe Cabacchi?"

"Do I? Oh, brother! What are you doing with them?"

"Nothing with them, but I'm trying to do something to them. Got any pictures of them around?"

"Dozens of them."

"Can I get one of each?"

"Sure. Come on down. I'll slip them in an envelope and meet you at the StakeOut."

"I'll be right down." I hung up and went out to my car. As

I pulled away from the curb, I noticed that once more I was being followed. It wasn't the same car, but I would have bet the same two men were in it. I drove down to Main Street and parked in the lot back of the StakeOut. It was a restaurant and bar owned by a retired police lieutenant good food, good drinks, and good companions most of the time.

My friend was already sitting at the bar. He had a drink in front of him and there was a martini in front of the empty stool next to him.

"How are you, Milo?" he asked warmly. "You still drinking martinis? I ordered one for you."

"Sure. How have you been, Jake?"

"Busy. We've all been working around the clock since the riot. You knew about that, didn't you?"

"I'm learning."

He slid a manila envelope over to me. "Here are the pictures. Is there a story in it?"

I opened the envelope and looked at the photos inside. They were good clear shots. "There's a story in it," I said. "A hell of a story. And it's right down your alley." He was the police reporter on his paper.

"Well?"

I shook my head. "Not yet, but I'll see that you get the jump on it. Should be very soon. That reminds me." I pulled out my address book and opened it to the page where I had copied down the number from the checkbook Masters had kept at home. "Does that remind you of a phone number or anything else?"

He looked at it. "Not a phone number," he said. He dragged

on his cigarette. "You know what it looks like to me? One of those Swiss bank numbers. You know, where you have a bank account under a number instead of your name? Yeah, I'm sure that's what it is. Where'd you get it?"

"I'll tell you later," I said. I had never thought of that as the answer, but it fit. I put my address book away. "Don't worry. I'll see that you get the whole story before anyone else does."

"Okay," he said.

I ordered two more drinks for us. I drank mine down fast. "I have to run, Jake. I'll be in touch. And thanks for the pictures."

He shrugged.

I left, got in my car, and headed back toward Hollywood. The tail was still with me.

This time I stopped and parked near the Boulevard Hotel. I noticed my tail parked three cars behind me. I went inside and up to the desk. The clerk put down his paperback book and came over.

"Yes, sir?"

"I'm an insurance investigator," I said. I showed him my ID. "Were you on duty the day Jimmy Altman was killed?"

A look of fear came into his eyes. "Yes, I was."

"Did you get a good look at the two men who ran out?"

"No, no, not a very good look. There was too much excitement."

I took the two photographs out and showed them to him. "Were these the two men?"

"No—I mean, I don't know. I didn't get a chance to really see them. They were running."

I knew he was lying. "Let's take an imaginary situation," I said. "Suppose you accidentally saw two suspected murderers leaving the scene of the crime. Suppose they were known criminals who had usually evaded the law. And suppose they either came around themselves or sent someone else to tell you that you'd better not remember them because something would happen to you if you did. It would be perfectly natural for you to be frightened and not want to identify them. Most of us would feel that way. But now suppose those same two men got into a position where they couldn't possibly carry out their threat and your testimony would make it certain they could never do anything like that again. Would you then change your mind and identify them?"

The sweat was running down his face as I talked, but I could see his attention fix on the last part of what I said. "Yes. Of course I would. I don't think criminals like that should be allowed to run around threatening people. Naturally, I would do everything I could. That is, in the imaginary situation you just mentioned."

"That's all I wanted to know," I said. "Thank you very much."

I went out to my car and drove on up the street to the Casa Del Monte and parked. I glanced at the other car as I crossed the sidewalk, but gave no sign of recognition. I didn't think they'd try anything where they might be seen by too many people, but I wasn't going to be foolish enough to close my eyes.

Inside the door of the bar, I stopped and waited until I adjusted to the dim lighting. Then I moved in the rest of the way. I saw the man I'd asked about, sitting at the bar. I went over and sat on the stool next to him. Bo brought me a gin and grapefruit and discreetly retired.

"He won't let me buy a drink," the man said. "Told me they were all on you."

"I told him to do that," I said. "I wanted to see you and thought you might have to wait. It was hardly fair to ask you to do that without also asking you to be my guest."

"It wasn't necessary, but thanks anyway. Did you see Al?"

"Yeah. He was helpful. But now I want to see him again or have you ask him one question for me and give me the answer."

"What is it?"

"He said that a man met him and picked up some supplies and paid for them for Jimmy Altman. He said the man was called Gino and his rough description fit a man I know by that name. I asked him if he would identify the man. He seemed very reluctant, but indicated that he might. He was obviously afraid that something would happen to him if he provided identification. I can understand that. But I'd like you to ask him if he would identify Gino providing he and his partner were in a position making it impossible for them to do anything to him."

"That sounds fair enough," Dean said. "I noticed there are some phone booths in the parking lot of the church across the street. I'll call him and come back with his answer."

"Okay," I said, "but just one thing. Do you know the man I'm talking about or does he know you?"

"Slightly. Why?"

"Then don't go out the front door. He and his partner are parked in front about three or four doors down. They're tailing me. Go out the back door and you can cross the street without being seen."

"Thanks."

He got up and moved toward the back. I turned to my drink. I had decided that it was about time that things were brought to a head. I thought I had the whole story—with only one piece missing out of the puzzle, so it was time to push.

I had almost finished my drink when Dean came back and took the stool next to me. "He said yes," he told me.

"Good. When the situation is ripe, do I get in touch with him through you? I won't tell the cops about him. Let him go in and volunteer the information."

"What will be his reason for that?"

I smiled. "If I'm right, their pictures will be in the newspapers. If I'm wrong, it may not make any difference. Either way, I'll try to catch you here. But if I don't, and you see their pictures in the paper, tell Al to go ahead. I'm pretty sure there'll be others coming in to tie the two men with Jimmy Altman. Okay?"

"Okay," he said.

I beckoned to Bo and gave him ten dollars, telling him to take out for the drinks. He rang them up and gave me the change. "Have another one before you go," he said, "on the house."

"No, thanks," I said. "I'll take a rain check. I just quit drinking—for at least two or three hours."

"What the hell are you going to do?" he asked.

"I have a date with destiny," I said. "At least, I think I do—unless I get stood up."

"You're out of your mind," Bo said. "You don't know what you're fooling with. ... Want me to go with you?"

"You're the one who doesn't know what he's fooling with," I said. "Besides, baby, this is my own bag. It's personal. I wouldn't take you along any more than I would take you with me to see the broad I'm going to see tonight. I may not be back later, but be sure you have plenty of grapefruit juice tomorrow. I may be thirsty."

I got up and walked out. I got into the car and drove up Hollywood Boulevard, looking back only once. About four blocks up, I turned left into a parking lot behind a row of buildings. The only way out of there was the same way I had entered, so I figured they wouldn't follow me in. Watching the rearview mirror, I saw that they had pulled to the curb across the street. I parked. From the lot there was an entrance to four stores. I went into the gun store.

"I want a twelve-gauge shotgun," I told the clerk. "Pump action. And a box of shells."

"Yes, sir," he said. He hesitated, looking at me. "I'll have to ask you for your name and address. It's a new policy."

"That's all right," I said. "My name is Milo March and I am presently living at the Continental Hotel. I'll also want some shells for a sidearm, a .38. I have a license for it, which should also serve as my identification for the other purchase." I pulled out my license and showed it to him.

He copied down the number of the license, my name, and the hotel. Then he brought me the shotgun. It was a good make. I told him I'd take it. He brought the shells for it and a box of .38 shells. I paid him and went back to the car. I put the shotgun under the front seat and the shells in the glove compartment. Then I went back to one of the other stores and bought three unimportant things. I tossed those on the front seat when I got back to the car, and drove out toward southeast Los Angeles. The other car dutifully followed.

I parked in front of the bar and went in. George was there with his friends, so I sat next to him. I told the bartender to give them drinks and to give me a Coke.

"Hey, man," George said, "you sick or something?"

"Nope," I said, "I'm in training. I have to make a couple of phone calls. I'll be right back." I left money on the bar and went to the phone booth in the back. My call was to Reno, station to station.

"Crooked Ted's," the voice said.

"Milo March," I said. "You sound as if you'd been chocking down quite a few."

"You know how it is, pal," he said. "What can I do for you?"

"I have one more question about Freddie," I answered. "Do you know if he ever broke his right leg?"

"That's a hell of a question," he said. "Wait a minute. There's someone here who might know." The phone was silent for a minute or two, then he came back on. "There's someone here who has known Freddie for a long time, and he says that he did break his right leg, but it was years ago when he was riding and before he became a trainer. What's going on?"

"I don't know for sure," I said, "but I think that Freddie may be dead. I'll let you know." I hung up, waited a minute, then put in a dime and called a local number.

"Mrs. Masters?" I asked when she answered.

"Yes. Who is speaking?"

"Milo March. I promised to call you about something."

"Yes?"

"About the stock in Belters, Incorporated. Don't buy it. I'll see that you know the full story very soon."

There was a pause. "Thank you, Mr. March," she said then.

I hung up and then dialed Sherry's number. She answered almost at once. "Hi, baby," I said. "Milo March."

"Hello, honey, I was wondering if I'd hear from you."

"Sure you will. Is it all right if I meet you tonight after the last show?"

"I'm not working tonight, honey."

"Good. Suppose I pick you up around eight or nine?"

"Make it nine," she said. "I'll be waiting for you."

I went back to the bar and my Coke. As I approached, one of George's friends was just coming back in from the street. He sat down and paid attention to his drink. I paid attention to my Coke. It wasn't too bad if you pretended there was some rum in it. But if it ever got out, I could just see the headlines: *Milo March Drinks Coke*. Wall Street would probably pull a 1929 all over again.

"What's with you, white man?" George asked. "I never seen you drinking that soft stuff before. You getting religion or something?"

"I told you. I'm in training. I'm going to take a little drive pretty soon and I don't want to get a five-zero-two."*

---

* A 502 is California police code for drunk driving.

"Yeah," he said. "How's the case coming along?"

"All right, I guess. We'll probably clean it up soon."

"Yeah," he said again. "You pushing?"

I looked at him. He was smart. I decided to level. "I'm pushing," I said. "It's the only way I know to bring things to a quick head."

"You got all the answers?"

"I have all but one. Now, I have to tie up what I've got and then find the one remaining answer. Nothing to it, baby."

He pushed his drink back on the bar. "Think I'll have a Coke," he told the bartender.

"What's with you?" I asked.

"Got a sweet tooth," he said. He looked at me. "Don't try to kid me, white boy. Those two honkies we all clashed with the other day—they got something to do with this, don't they?"

"They have something to do with it," I admitted.

"They're like maybe key figures. If there's enough pressure on them, they might be the weak links."

"They might be."

"So they're the ones you're pushing. You've been pushing them; now you've got them to the point where they're ready to flip. Right?"

"Maybe."

"They're outside right now," he said, "in a different car. Which means they're ready to push back. And you know it and that's why you're drinking Coke. Right?"

"Maybe," I said.

"You know," he went on, "that they won't try to kill you where there will be fifty or a hundred witnesses, and you know they are going to stay on your tail now until they think they have a break. So you're going to hang around just long enough and then lead them to where they think they'll have a break."

"I don't know what you're talking about," I said.

"You know, white boy. You're going to take them out somewhere so they'll make a try for you. Then you're planning on taking them. I don't know how you're going to work it, but that's the idea."

"So what?" I said.

"I'm going with you," he said.

I shook my head. "No, George. You don't understand, but this is something personal. I have to do it myself."

"You don't understand," he said. His voice was low but intense. "You told me your idea of what happened down here in that one fire. When you did that, you make it something personal to me. You can't take that away from me any more than I can take your feeling away from you. I think I know some of the things you feel. You must know some of the things I feel. I'm telling you, man, you and I are in this together."

"But—" I started.

"I don't know what it is exactly, Milo, but if you believe in any kind of integration, this is it. There ain't going to be any segregation here at this moment. I go with you or nobody goes."

I was silent, taking in what he had said.

"If you don't let me go with you," he continued, "then you ain't going. I'm here and I've got five friends with me. You got a gun, but you can't get rid of all of us. You take your stand right here, boy. You're either for integration or segregation. Once you make a choice, it goes for both life and death. You started the game, baby, and now it's your play."

I looked at him and I knew he was right. "Okay, George," I said. "You can come. I was just trying to keep you out of trouble."

"You can't do that, man. I'm already in trouble. I was in trouble from the day I was born, because my skin is black. I'm in trouble because I had something to do with that riot. When you try to protect me when it gets rough, you're just playing Massa to the black slave. I don't need that. You don't need it. If I'm fit to live with you, then I am also fit to die with you. If I'm not fit to live with you, then to hell with dying with you. Baby, it's integration all the way or it's nothing at all."

"You're right," I said. "Give us two more Cokes and give those other gentlemen some good whiskey."

"Okay," George said, and I could feel him relax. "What's the program?"

"How the hell do I know?" I said irritably. "I don't have any program. I never do. I just play the cards the way they fall. I think the two hoods are ripe. They've been pushed about as far as their egos will permit. To top it off, they have a pretty good idea of some of the things I've been working on. You saw they're driving a different car today. I think that means they'll try to hit me if they can catch me in a vulnerable position. All I can do is give them the chance and see what happens. It might be a dry run and nothing will happen."

"So we'll find out," he said. He sounded happy.

"You see," I said, "you are also an unknown factor in this."

"What do you mean?"

"They might decide they don't want to try to take two men, whereas one man would be a cinch. On the other hand, the sight of you might just make them more eager to kill both of us. And the fact that you already have one bullet hole in you will make it seem easier."

"When do we go?"

"In an hour or so. Let them get more eager and more tensed up. That way, they'll make more mistakes."

So we sat and drank Cokes and talked about other things. I never drank so many Cokes in my life. Finally I couldn't stand the thought of another one.

"Let's go," I said. "And try to act as if we don't know we're being followed. It might make them a little overconfident."

We went out and climbed into the Cadillac. As we drove off, I saw the other car dutifully fall in behind us.

"Do you know how to use a shotgun, George?"

"Do I? Man, just turn me loose with one."

"There's one right under the front seat. Don't lift it high enough for them to see it."

He reached down and brought up the gun, resting it across his lap. "It's a beauty."

"There's a box of shells in the glove compartment."

He got out the shells and loaded the gun.

"The other box," I said, "contains ammo for my .38. Take out a handful and give them to me." He did, and I dropped them in my pocket.

We had been driving west. When we reached Coldwater

Canyon, I turned to the right. The other car followed. I didn't drive fast, but kept at the steady pace of a man who knows where he's going.

"One more thing, George," I said. "I don't want you to use that unless you absolutely have to. Let me do the shooting unless it looks like someone is going to get me. And if you shoot, don't shoot to kill. Aim for a foot or a leg. The range will be close enough to do sufficient damage. I want both of them alive, but in bad condition. Think you can do it?"

He laughed. "Man, I spent a year in Vietnam. They didn't teach me to knit sweaters." He rolled down his window. "How do you think they'll make their play? Passing us? If so, I'd better get in the back seat."

"I don't think so," I said. "They can't be sure of accuracy that way. I think they'll pass us pretty soon and then try to set up an ambush. Anyway, if you climb into the back seat now, it would be a tip-off. I may be wrong, but let's take a gamble that I'm right."

"They're your dice, baby. I'll bet with you."

We finally reached a spot where there was no turning off until we reached the Valley. The road here twisted and turned, so it was ideal for a booby trap and there was very little traffic. I noticed that the car behind us was speeding up, so it looked as if I'd guessed right. I slipped my gun from the holster just in case they did make a try as they passed us.

They swept by us without even glancing in our direction and disappeared around the next curve. When we rounded it, they were still out of sight.

"It'll be any minute now," I said. "I imagine they'll block

the road with their car. I'll make a fast stop and roll out on this side. They're pros, so there will probably be one on each side of us. You worry about the one on your side."

"Okay."

We rounded three more curves—and there they were. It was a good spot. You could see far enough in both directions to be warned if anyone was coming. Their car was across the road, blocking it. I got a quick glimpse of one of them on my side of the road and the other one crouched down on the other side.

I hit the brakes and threw the car in neutral. The tires squealed. Then, at what I hoped was the right time, I yanked on the emergency brake and threw open my door. I tumbled out, my gun in my hand, and rolled as I hit the ground. I heard two shots, but I wasn't paying too much attention. When I stopped rolling, I was lying on my belly facing Gino Benetto. I steadied my gun, ignoring everything else. There was another shot and something plucked at the shoulder of my coat. I got the gun sight where I wanted it and gently squeezed the trigger.

I saw his trousers jump at the knee and knew I'd hit the mark even before he screamed. He dropped his gun and fell to the ground, clutching at a bloody kneecap. The shotgun roared behind me.

Benetto was flopping around on the ground, and every time he breathed it was a scream. But he was still trying to pick up his gun and he finally succeeded. I took aim again and pulled the trigger. I got the other kneecap. Benetto fainted in the middle of the next scream.

I looked around. Cabacchi was also on the ground, and I

could see that his right foot was mostly in shreds. He was flopping around and groaning, but he wasn't trying to recover his gun. I stood up and looked at George. He was climbing out of the car, the shotgun in his hand.

"I think he's had enough," I said, "but watch him." I turned and looked down the winding road leading to the Valley. There was a car coming toward us. We could send them to call the police. I leaned against the Cadillac and suddenly felt tired.

TEN

It wasn't too long before the sirens were wailing. The two policemen and an ambulance arrived at about the same time. They took one look at the two men on the ground and hurriedly loaded them into the ambulance, while the cops watched us, guns drawn.

"All right," one of them said, as the ambulance pulled away, "who are you and what's this all about?"

"My name is Milo March," I said. "This is my friend George Henderson. I'm an insurance investigator. Those two men were involved in a case I'm working on. They blocked the road, as you can see, and tried to kill us when we had to stop. I don't know if you recognized them, but they are both professional killers."

"Doesn't look like they were so professional this time," the cop said dryly. His gun was in his hand and he was watching both of us. "Where are the guns?"

"The small gun is in my holster," I said. "The shotgun is in the car. I own both guns and the hand gun is registered. I have a permit for it."

"That's nice, but I'll take the guns and then we'll all go downtown."

"Do you know Lieutenant Whitmore?" I asked.

"I know him. What about it?"

"Call him on the radio. Tell him what's happened and who you have, and tell him I want to talk to him."

He looked doubtful, but I could tell he also didn't want to take any chances on making a mistake. "Keep your gun on both of them," he told the other officer. "If they make a move, shoot them." He went to his police car.

A few minutes later, he stuck his head out of the car window. "Hey, March," he called. "Come here."

I walked over to him. "The Lieutenant wants to talk to you," he said curtly. He handed me the phone.

"Hello, Lieutenant," I said.

"March," he said, "what the hell is going on?"

"Benetto and Cabacchi tried to ambush me. It didn't quite work out that way. They're both in bad shape, but they'll live."

"Why did they try?"

"You know the case I'm working on. And it ties in with the murder in the Boulevard Hotel. They wanted to get rid of me. I think I can guarantee, however, that you can have them on a silver platter."

"All right, but you still have to come in and make a statement. Who's the spade with you?"

"A friend of mine. We'll both be there within an hour and make our statements."

"Why the hell don't you stay in New York instead of coming out here and trying to run the police department? All right, but you'd better be here within an hour or I'll have the whole force after you. Put the officer back on."

"He wants to talk to you," I told the cop, handing him the phone.

He took it and listened for a couple of minutes. Then he said, "Yes, sir."

He hung up and turned back to me. "Okay. You can go, but you're to be in Lieutenant Whitmore's office in an hour."

"Thanks, officer. I'll be there."

He was staring at my left shoulder. "Wait a minute. Are you wounded?"

I glanced down where there was a jagged tear in my jacket. "No," I said. "I guess a bullet ripped some threads. That's all."

I walked back to the car and nodded to George. "Let's go," I said.

We got into the Cadillac. The other car was still blocking the way down to the Valley. I turned around and we went back the way we had come, except this time I drove faster. I went straight to my hotel. I told the attendant I'd want the car again in about thirty minutes. Then we went upstairs.

The bottle of V.O. was almost gone. I lifted it and drank about half of what was left, then handed the bottle to George. I called room service and told them to send up another bottle and a bucket of ice. Then I made another call—to the Stake-Out. I asked for Jake. He was still there.

"Jake," I said, "this is Milo March. This is a partial payoff; the big story will come later. Remember the two men we talked about?"

"Who could forget them?"

"They were shot in Coldwater Canyon less than an hour ago. They tried to ambush me and were shot by me and a friend of mine. I think they'll live, but it'll be a long time before they can walk. This is one rap I don't think they can beat. And there will be other raps against them. The police took them to a hospital. I don't know where, but you can probably find out without any trouble. My friend and I will be with Lieutenant Whitmore in a few minutes to make statements. And, Jake, try to play it up as much as you can—with pictures of them and a little emphasis on how long it'll be before they can walk and how little chance they have of beating this."

"Will do," he said. "Thanks, Milo."

"Wait until the big plum."

I hung up just as a knock sounded on the door. I let the waiter in and signed the bill. He left and I poured myself a big drink on ice. "Have to get the taste of those Cokes out of my mouth," I said. "There's another glass in the bathroom. Help yourself."

George went to get the glass. I downed my drink, then stood up and stripped off my jacket. The side of my shirt was all red.

"Hey," George said, "you got hit."

"No," I said. "I cut myself shaving this morning."

I ripped off the shirt and went into the bathroom. I washed the blood off and looked at my shoulder. There was a small furrow across the top of it—not too deep. It was still bleeding slightly, but not much. I went back into the room and picked up the bottle of V.O.

"That don't look too good," George said. "Maybe you'd better see a doctor."

"Can't stand doctors," I said. I uncorked the bottle and poured some whiskey on my shoulder. It burned like hell.

"It may make me smell like a drunk, but it'll kill the germs. There's some Band-Aids in the bathroom. Get them, will you, and cover me up?"

He brought back the Band-Aids and put on three of them. I changed to another suit and a clean shirt, took another fast drink, and looked at him.

"Let's go. The Lieutenant is waiting."

He was, too. For once he wasn't sitting at his desk. He was pacing back and forth in his small office.

"Lieutenant," I said, "this is my friend George Henderson."

"Hello," he said shortly. "March, what the hell is this?"

"I told you. They ambushed us and tried to shoot it out. How are they?"

"They're okay. There's some doubt whether Benetto will ever walk again, and Cabacchi will always have a limp."

"So you have them for assault with intent to commit homicide for a starter. And believe me, that's only a starter. I think you'll now get your identifications in the murder of Jimmy Altman. And within forty-eight hours I think I can guarantee that you'll also be able to charge them with the murder of three John Does, arson, conspiracy to commit murder and arson, conspiracy to commit fraud, and probably a few other little things."

"What are you talking about?"

"I'll give you the whole story on the other things later."

"What do you mean, later!" he asked indignantly.

"First things first," I said.

"Make a statement now and file a complaint against them."

He nodded, as if agreeing that came first.

"Yes," I said.

"Okay. Those other three murders you mentioned—are you referring to the three men who died in the Belters fire?"

"Yes. I think you can safely say that the three men were Larry Beld, Bob Summers, and—Freddie Freeman."

"Who the hell is he?"

"A wino from Reno, Nevada. Masters brought him back here a few days before the fire and made him the clean-up man for the building—a job Masters created out of thin air. Freeman hasn't been seen since the day of the fire. You can get a rundown on him and his connection with Masters through the Reno police."

"You mean Masters didn't die in the fire?"

"That's exactly what I believe."

"Where is he?"

"I'm not sure, but I expect to be able to produce him in forty-eight hours."

"All right," he said with a sigh, "let's take one thing at a time. You'll make a statement and sign a complaint. Right?"

"I told you so."

He got a police stenographer, and George and I made our statements and signed them. The complaint was drawn up and I signed that. Then we were finally allowed to leave because I refused to say anything more until I could produce Masters.

"Was all that on the level?" George asked as we drove southeast.

"On the level," I said. I was tired and my shoulder was hurting.

"You were saying that old man Masters is still alive."

"I think we could safely bet on it."

"You know where he is?"

"I think I know. I'll have to come up with more than that in the next two days. Just one thing, George."

"What's that?"

"Button up about it. Not a word to anyone until you hear from me."

"Okay."

I drove to the bar and went in with him for a couple of drinks—no Cokes this time. Then I went back to the hotel, had another stiff drink, and went to sleep.

I felt a little better when I awakened that evening, but my shoulder was still hurting. I got ready for my date. I picked up Sherry at nine and we went out to dinner. I made sure that we were back at her apartment early. We fixed a couple of drinks, after which she got comfortable, and then we retired to the living room. She suddenly wanted to talk about my job, but I asked her if we could catch the late news first.

She pulled me into the bedroom and turned on the television, before going back to the kitchen to make fresh drinks. By the time she'd returned, the news was on.

There were a couple of other stories first, then they got to the shooting in Coldwater Canyon. They showed pictures of the spot where it had happened and shots of the two men in a prison hospital. There were no pictures of me, but I was mentioned at some length.

I was watching Sherry while the story was on. Her face tightened at the first mention of Benetto and Cabacchi, and she watched the screen without once looking at me. When it was finally over, I got up and turned the set off.

"That's what my job is like," I said gently.

"It—it must be difficult," she answered. She got up, and went out to make another drink for herself.

This night was different than the other nights. She had five more French seventy-fives in about a half hour, and suddenly slumped in a chair, passed out. I lifted her and put her on the bed. Then I let myself out and went to my hotel. I went to sleep at once.

I was up by seven o'clock. The shoulder hurt, but it looked all right. I phoned room service and ordered breakfast and some more ice. I had a drink and ate breakfast; then I called Martin Raymond.

"Milo, boy," he said when he came on, "how are things going? I see by the paper you were mixed up in something out there. Have to do with our case?"

"Yeah. It's all wrapped up and your money saved—except for one final little item. I want you to telegraph me another thousand dollars as soon as you hang up."

"What?" he shouted. "We've already given you two thousand dollars, and you just said the case is all wrapped up."

"Except for one thing," I said gently. "Watch your blood pressure, Martin. The final, and necessary, proof depends on producing Harry Masters alive. If anything gets out about this, he'll simply vanish again. So I'm going after him—to Europe. That's the reason for the extra thousand dollars."

"All right," he said wearily. "I'll see that it's sent off at once. You'll let me know?"

"Right away," I said.

I hung up and called an airline. I made a reservation on a plane for Paris, then I phoned Lieutenant Whitmore.

I briefly outlined the case for him, telling him that I thought I knew where Masters was, but I didn't know what name he was using. I would find him, get the police to arrest him, and then it would be up to him. But I warned him not to let anything leak out.

"Now, one more thing. There's a stripper named Sherry LaSalle who's involved. She passed out last night after hearing about Benetto and Cabacchi. I know that she had been in contact with them. Benetto's phone number is in her address book. She probably also knows how to reach Masters. I suggest that you pick her up on suspicion of being in conspiracy with both men concerning the attack on me in Coldwater. Just keep her out of circulation for forty-eight hours."

"All right," he said sourly. "When are you planning on taking over the whole department?"

"Not me," I said. "It doesn't pay enough. I'll call you from Europe."

I hung up and then called Jake's newspaper. He was there.

"I don't have much time, Jake," I said, "but I can meet you at the StakeOut for a few minutes."

"I'll be there," he said.

I got dressed and packed my suitcase. Downstairs I stopped long enough to tell them that I was expecting a telegram and would be back for it, also that I would be gone for two days, but I was keeping the room.

On the way downtown I sold the shotgun at a gun store I had passed. Then I went to the StakeOut. Jake was there, with a drink waiting for me. I gave him an outline of the whole case. He whistled softly when I'd finished.

"Twenty-two million dollars and four murders," Jake said. "That's quite a story. You want me to sit on it, is that right?"

"Until I get Masters. I'll call you from Europe."

"Okay. It's a deal."

I went back to my hotel. The telegram had just arrived, so I took the money order to a Western Union office and cashed it, before driving out to International Airport. I made arrangements to park the car and picked up my ticket, then waited in the cocktail lounge until my flight was called.

The trip was like all such trips. There was good food, good drinks, pretty girls, a mediocre movie, and a lot of clouds. I slept as much as I could. Eventually we landed in Paris.

I went through the authorities and arranged to get a plane to Monte Carlo. It was a small plane and a short flight. When I arrived, I went directly to a hotel. I shaved, took a shower, and changed clothes. Then I went down to investigate the bar.

Monte Carlo is a famous place, but it is also a small one. If Masters was there, I was sure I'd run into him. He'd certainly go to the casino, and it was right next door to this hotel. He was probably staying here. All I had to do was be patient.

I had a couple of drinks and then wandered over to the casino. I had some luck.

Masters was leaving with a beautiful young girl just as I entered. There was no mistaking that face. I went on by, played roulette for a few minutes, losing only a small amount of money, then went back to the bar. He and the girl were sitting there. I managed to sit close to them.

"How are the tables running?" I asked in my best French when the bartender brought my martini.

He laughed. "You should ask that gentleman," he said, indicating Masters. "He is the big winner this week."

"What did he say?" I heard Masters ask the girl.

"The gentleman ask how were the tables," she said. Her English was not too good. "He say ask you. You big winner."

In English I said. "I congratulate you, sir. May I buy you and your lady a drink?"

He nodded reluctantly. I gave the order to the bartender and he served them.

"Thank you, sir," Masters said. "You are an American?"

"Yes. Milo March from New York City."

"I'm Mark Harris," he said. "From Chicago. The young lady is Claudette Chambrun."

"Nice to meet you," I said. I noticed that he had kept his initials, only reversing them, for his new name.

We indulged in some more small talk and then I excused myself. I didn't want to push it too fast. I bought a paper and went up to my room, and stayed there until dinnertime.

I saw them again in the dining room, but I merely bowed and went on to my table.

After dinner I went to the bar for a brandy. Then I went to the casino. He was already there, playing. I managed to get near him, and smiled and nodded. I noticed that he was winning again. I started out with a strong winning streak, which I pushed as much as I could. At the end of two hours, I had a great pile of chips in front of me. I decided to quit while I was ahead. I went over and cashed in. I had won almost ten thousand dollars. I hoped it was a good omen.

Masters was heading for the cashier as I left. I went to the bar and ordered a drink, aware that Masters and the girl came in a few minutes later and took a table.

A little later a waiter came to me. "The gentleman and lady asked if you would care to join them at their table."

"Tell them I will be delighted," I said. "And bring us three drinks."

I walked over to the table. Masters stood up.

"It was very nice of you," I said, "to invite me to join you."

"Not at all," he said. "I know it gets lonely here sometimes when you're from the States."

That was the one thing I was counting on. He'd probably be missing a lot of things he was accustomed to. I didn't think he'd be too suspicious, because he probably thought he had pulled off a foolproof job. I hadn't pushed myself on him, so now he was seeking my company.

We exchanged a few remarks about both of us winning. Then he asked me what line I was in. I told him insurance, that I had my own company and was on vacation. He confided that he was in real estate back in Chicago and was also on vacation. And so it went. I noticed he was drinking heavily. I finally excused myself early and went to my room.

I was down early the next morning and went to the dining room for breakfast. I had a drink in front of me and was waiting for my meal when he came in alone. I waved to him and asked why he didn't join me. He seemed glad that I had asked.

A drink before breakfast?" he asked as he sat down.

"Yes. I find that it gives me a better appetite."

"Maybe that's a good idea," he said. He ordered a drink and some food. "You're up a little early, aren't you, Mr. March?"

"No, I usually get up early. Then I was thinking about going to Paris today. I like the gambling here, but otherwise it's a little boring."

"It's not the season," he said. "And it is a little dull. I was even thinking of a trip to Paris myself."

"Good," I said. "Why don't you come with me? I have a suite reserved there and you can be my guest."

"Know any girls in Paris?" he asked.

"Lots of them. Why don't you come along?"

"I think I will," he said.

"Fine. I'll make the flight reservations after breakfast and we'll be there in time for lunch. If we get bored, we can always come back and gamble."

He nodded, seeming pleased by the whole idea. As soon as I finished my breakfast I went to arrange for the flight, telling him I'd see him in the bar later.

After making the plane reservations I called a hotel suggested by the clerk and reserved a suite. I walked around outside for a while, and then I went upstairs and packed my things before returning to the bar.

Masters came in a few minutes later. "Well, I'm ready," he said.

"Me, too," I answered. "Have a drink, then we'll have the boy bring down our luggage and we'll be on our way."

We sent for our luggage a few minutes later, and were in a

taxi on our way to Paris, when he began to get excited about the whole project.

In Paris, we took a taxi to the hotel. It was a pretty fancy place, and the suite was even fancier. I could see he was impressed.

"Now," I said, "we'll go to lunch."

I remembered several good spots from other trips I had made to the city, so I knew where to take him. But first we stopped off at the New York Bar and had a few drinks. He was delighted with the place. Finally we went on to a restaurant where we had lunch with plenty of wine. He wanted to go back to the New York Bar, where we spent most of the afternoon. I kept encouraging him to have more to drink. I was getting the glimmer of an idea.

When we finally left the bar, he was feeling no pain. We took a taxi back to the hotel.

"What about girls?" he asked when we were in the suite.

"It's too early yet," I said. "We'll have a couple more drinks, and then get some rest before we pick up the girls."

"Good idea," he muttered.

I called room service and ordered a couple bottles of whiskey and some soda and ice. A waiter brought them up in a few minutes. I poured a glass almost full of whiskey and added a little soda. Then I poured a little whiskey and a lot of soda in another glass. I gave him the first one and took the second for myself.

"Mark," I said, "let's drink to Paris."

He was half asleep, but he revived enough to lift his glass. "To Paris."

"Bottoms up," I said.

He nodded wisely, tipped the glass, and didn't stop until he'd finished it.

I took it and quickly refilled it, putting it back in his hand.

"Now let's drink to the girls of Paris," I said. "Down the hatch."

"Girls," he said, but I could hardly understand him.

He made an effort and emptied that glass. When he'd finished, he stared blankly at it until it slipped from his fingers. Then he bent over slowly and fell to the floor. He was out.

I unbuttoned the collar of his shirt, twisted up his tie, and pulled his coat half off him. I went around and carefully wrecked the whole room, breaking lamps and a couple of chairs, and tossing all the bedding on the floor. Then I poured some whiskey over him and on the floor. I went back to my side of the suite and called the manager of the hotel.

"I am sorry," I said, "but I think my friend has had too much to drink this afternoon. I'm afraid he's torn up his room. Will you please come up?"

The manager was there so fast he must have run up the stairs instead of taking the elevator. He took one look at the room and began to scream in French so rapidly I could barely follow him. He was going to call the police; we would both go to jail and never get out—plus a general rundown on our ancestry.

I waited until he ran out of breath. "You're right," I told him. "I think you should call the police—at once."

He looked at me in astonishment.

"I will pay you for the damages," I said, "as soon as I go to the bank tomorrow. But I'm afraid he might wake up later and do more damage. It is better that you call the police. They can lock him up and keep him overnight. Tomorrow morning he will be sober and very sorry for what he did. Then, tomorrow, as soon as I pay you for the damages, the police will let him go."

He thought about that for a moment and liked it. The police could hold my friend until I paid for the damage. He brightened up at once and went to phone the police.

They came very soon. It was impossible to awaken Masters, so they ended up carrying him off to jail. I reassured the manager that I would pay, and he went to great length to tell me that he knew I was a gentleman and would do so, but he kept emphasizing that my friend would be out of jail when I paid. I'd heard him tell the police not to let Masters out until they heard from the hotel. I finally managed to get the manager out of the room.

I sat down and had a short drink. Then I picked up the phone and went to work. I first called Lieutenant Whitmore in Los Angeles.

"Masters is in a Paris jail," I told him when he answered. "The charge is only disorderly conduct and the destruction of property, but he'll be there for at least twelve hours. I think I can guarantee that. He's using the name Mark Harris. But you'd better move quickly to see that he's held for an extradition hearing. I'll come back to Los Angeles tomorrow and give you all the additional facts I have."

"You'd better," he said grimly.

Next, I called Martin Raymond in New York. I told him that the case was wrapped up and his money saved, and explained I was coming straight back, but that I'd have to stay in Los Angeles long enough to appear at an arraignment. He was so happy that he mumbled hysterically about a bonus for me. I hung up while he was thinking about that.

I made one more call—to Marie Lester, Masters's secretary in Los Angeles. "This is Milo March," I said. "I'm in Paris."

"You're where?" she gasped.

"Paris. I just thought I'd tell you it's over."

"You mean—we will all be out of work?"

"I think so, honey, but don't tell anyone yet. I'm taking a plane back tomorrow and I'll see you over the best dinner in town."

I hung up and realized that last sentence had made me feel hungry. I went downstairs and had dinner all by myself.

AFTERWORD

The March Method

There are twenty-two full-length novels in the Milo March series, plus a handful of stories. Sometimes mystery buffs who have read one or two of the novels expect Milo to work by means of deduction from clues at the crime scene or other physical evidence. I've read a number of reviews that either complained that there was "no detection" in a novel or praised it for having "more detection than usual."

But, as Milo explains in many of the books, his method is not like that of other detectives: "All this business about deduction is a lot of nonsense. There are only two ways to solve a case. One is by plugging hard work, and that's not for me. The other is to start pushing and wait to see who pushes back. That's my system, and it's always worked pretty well."

Milo might say to those reviewers, "You've been reading too many books, honey. I don't go around looking for clues. I just sit around, sometimes drinking as much brandy as I can, and let things drift in my direction. Whatever comes to me, I investigate."

Milo's method is intrinsic to his character and temperament. He works instinctively, without a definite strategy, waiting for events to ripen, then springing into action at the right moment. Patience, Milo believes, is one of the best qualities a detective can have. "Besides," he says, "I'm getting too old to chase miscreants down the street. It's easier to let them chase me down the street."

Sometimes Milo claims that he doesn't like to work; he would prefer to spend his time downing his favorite beverages in the company of a beautiful, intelligent woman. But he works because he likes the money ($300 a day in 1960s dollars): "It comes in handy when I want to add to my stamp collection."

On the other hand, Milo also claims that when he's on a case, he is *always* working. He's done some of his best skull work while sitting at a bar, for example:

> Joe brought a martini without being told. "You working?" he asked as he set it down.
>
> "Of course, I'm working," I said indignantly. "I'm always working. It's brain work. That's why it doesn't show."

The success of this approach seems to be a combination of two things. Number one, Milo gathers information about the people involved in the crime and consults his own intuition about what probably happened. After poking around a bit—even if as simply as by chatting up the locals in a bar—he allows things to take their natural course. In brief, the March Method—start pushing and see who pushes back. Number two, he focuses mental attention on the case, without making a firm conclusion, and then goofs off, letting the brain do its work unconsciously: "I had a cup of coffee, then a drink,  and finally stretched out on the bed. I thought about the case and fell asleep." (One reviewer did suggest that we need not be told about every time Milo stretched out on the bed.)

It sounds like a rather passive approach, but only up to a point. As things progress, Milo starts to feel nervous or excited; then he knows his efforts are bearing fruit. Spontaneously, he springs into action.

"Don't start anything."
"I never start things. I only finish them."

Like his predecessor, the Green Lama—the Buddhist pulp superhero that Ken Crossen created in the 1940s—Milo prefers to avoid violence. But he almost always carries a couple of firearms, usually with a permit. Although the average person can't spot a gun in a shoulder holster, people are always commenting on the bulge under Milo's coat.

"Carrying your gun?"

"That's right."

"Why?"

I smiled at him. "I've never discovered a way to catch bullets in my teeth. If someone is going to shoot at me, I want to be able to shoot back."

That's his .38. For extra assurance, Milo relies on an old four-barreled derringer that he had rebored so it would take a .32. He had a little harness made for it so it would clip under the edge of his coat. "It worked something like a magician's gimmick; all I had to do was press my arm against the clip, and the tiny gun would drop into my hand." Those four shots come in handy many a time.

Milo has taken a few bullets. He's also killed a few weasel-faced hoods who were pointing guns at him, sometimes from a moving vehicle, and he didn't always tell the cops about it either. Rarely, he kills a man who "merely needs it." ("I pulled the trigger. The nastiness was suddenly gone from his face and there was blood in its place. It looked better that way.") But Milo is not hired to kill. He says, "I kill someone when it is necessary to save my own life. Even then, if I have time, I try to wound them."

Aside from such principles, March just knows what he wants in a rough way and doesn't map it out any more carefully than that. He never knows when he may have to change direction on a dime, like the time Milo is about to rescue an American captive in Russia, having knocked several officials briefly unconscious, and the guy says he won't go!*

Not insisting on a complete outline seems like wise advice—in insurance investigation, in life … and even in writing novels, where the few surviving plot synopses by Ken Crossen show that while he did plan in a complete way, last-minute variations could creep into the final work.**

I can't think of an argument to refute this explanation of Milo's:

"When you're looking for a needle in a haystack, you can't draw a picture showing which way the needle's pointing. All you can do is keep on sitting down all over the place until finally you get the point."

Kendra Crossen Burroughs

---

* This occurs in one of the short stories "in *The Twisted Trap,* #23 in this series.
** An example is reproduced in the back of *Death to the Brides,* #22 in this series.

ABOUT THE AUTHOR

Kendell Foster Crossen (1910–1981), the only child of Samuel Richard Crossen and Clo Foster Crossen, was born on a farm outside Albany in Athens County, Ohio—a village of some 550 souls in the year of this birth. His ancestors on his mother's side include the 19th-century songwriter Stephen Collins Foster ("Oh! Susanna"); William Allen, founder of Allentown, Pennsylvania; and Ebenezer Foster, one of the Minute Men who sprang to arms at the Lexington alarm in April 1775.

Ken went to Rio Grande College on a football scholarship but stayed only one year. "When I was fairly young, I developed the disgusting habit of reading," says Milo March, and it seems Ken Crossen, too, preferred self-education. He loved literature and poetry; favorite authors included Christopher Marlowe and Robert Service. He also enjoyed participant sports and was a semi-pro fighter in the heavyweight class. He became a practicing magician and had a passion for chess.

After college Ken wrote several one-act plays that were produced in a small Cleveland theater. He worked in steel mills and Fisher Body plants. Then he was employed as an insurance investigator, or "claims adjuster," in Cleveland. But he left the job and returned to the theater, now as a performer: a tumbling clown in the Tom Mix Circus; a comic and carnival barker for a tent show, and an actor in a medicine show.

In 1935, Ken hitchhiked to New York City with a typewriter under his arm, and found work with the WPA Writers' Project, covering cricket for the *New York City Guidebook*. In 1936, he was hired by the Munsey Publishing Company as associate editor of the popular *Detective Fiction Weekly*. The company asked him to come up with a character to compete with The Shadow, and thus was born a unique superhero of pulps, comic books, and radio—The Green Lama, an American mystic trained in Tibetan Buddhism.

Crossen sold his first story, "The Aaron Burr Murder Case," to *Detective Fiction Weekly* in September 1939, but says he didn't begin to make a living from writing till 1941. He tried his hand at publishing true crime magazines, comics, and a picture magazine, without great success, so he set out for Hollywood. From his typewriter flowed hundreds of stories, short novels for magazines, scripts radio, television, and film, nonfiction articles. He delved into science fiction in the 1950s, starting with "Restricted Clientele" (February 1951). His dystopian novels *Year of Consent* and *The Rest Must Die* also appeared in this decade.

In the course of his career Ken Crossen acquired six pseudonyms: Richard Foster, Bennett Barlay, Kent Richards, Clay Richards, Christopher Monig, and M.E. Chaber. The variety was necessary because different publishers wanted to reserve specific bylines for their own publications. Ken based "M.E. Chaber" on the Hebrew word for "author," *mechaber.*

In the early '50s, as M.E. Chaber, Crossen began to write a series of full-length mystery/espionage novels featuring Milo March, an insurance investigator. The first, *Hangman's Harvest,* was published in 1952. In all, there are twenty-two Milo March novels. One, *The Man Inside,* was made into a British film starring Jack Palance.

Most of Ken's characters were private detectives, and Milo was the most popular. Paperback Library reissued twenty-five Crossen titles in 1970–1971, with covers by Robert McGinnis. Twenty were Milo March novels, four featured an insurance investigator named Brian Brett, and one was about CIA agent Kim Locke.

Crossen excelled at producing well-plotted entertainment with fast-moving action. His research skills were a strong asset, back when research meant long hours searching library microfilms and poring over street maps and hotel floorplans. His imagination took him to many international hot spots, although he himself never traveled abroad. Like Milo March, he hated flying ("When you've seen one cloud, you've seen them all").

Ken Crossen was married four times. With his first wife he had three children (Stephen, Karen, Kendra) and with his second a son (David). He lived in New York, Florida, Southern California, Nevada, and other parts of the country. Milo March moves from Denver to New York City after five books of the series, with an apartment on Perry Street in Greenwich Village; that's where Ken lived, too. His and Milo's favorite watering hole was the Blue Mill Tavern, a short walk from the apartment.

Ken Crossen was a combination of many of the traits of his different male characters: tough, adventuresome, with a taste for gin and shapely women. But perhaps the best observation was made in an obituary written by sci-fi writer Avram David-son, who described Ken as a fundamentally gentle person who had been buffeted by many winds.